Why He Married Her & Played Me

Nine Secrets To What He's Thinking

PRESENTED BY

P. Koffe Brown

Destined for Greatness Publishing Group Printed in the United States of America

ISBN: 978-0-578-76108-4

Book Design by P. Koffe Brown

Please enjoy our first publication titled "The Race to the Ring, The Seven Seas of a Successful Courtship."

https://www.amazon.com/Race-Ring-Seven-Successful-Courtship/dp/0578630656

Be on the lookout for our next book coming Spring 2021

"She Chose Him & Screwed Me! Nine Reasons for Her Decision".

CONTENTS

Acknowledgements 1

Introduction 6

Marriage Is Honorable............................ 15

Chapter 1: She Learned Me To Earn Me........... 23

Chapter 2: You Never Gave Him A Reason To
Commit.. 38

Chapter 3: You're A Placeholder, Not A Partner52

Chapter 4: You Were Not Marriage Material..... 73

Chapter 5: She Did Not Need A Man; She Wanted
A Man.. 91

Chapter 6: He Wasn't Ready 104

Chapter 7: Sexual Compatibility 120

Chapter 8: Social Compatibility 138

Chapter 9: Spiritual Connection 163

The Conclusion Of The Matter...................... 184

Acknowledgements

I want to thank you, the reader, for picking up this book and enjoying the pages. If it were not for you, then writing for me would be in vain. I certainly want to thank God for blessing me with this unique idea to bring the value of healthy relationships to the forefront of all our minds. Next, I must thank **LOVE** for leading me to have a desire to share this type of connection with another human being. I also must thank my parents for creating me and showing me the power of loving one human being for life! I have never seen two people fight so hard to lead a life that shows the magic of partnership, purpose, patience, persistence, and passion. You two are a real-life example that all things are possible in a relationship if you believe!

I would also like to thank the humans I have created Myles, Maya, and Yasmin Mone't. The three of you push me to win. Thank you for being my children and my reason **WHY**!

You guys are making me into a **"DOPE BILLIONAIRE MOM."** I enjoy being your mother. It has made me a much better woman. I love you, and always remember that you are my greatest gift!

Finally, I would be remised if I did not thank the other contributing authors and the fantastic editor on this project. As I began to think and consider the pages of this book, your names came to mind. For some reason beyond my understanding, you said YES without hesitation. For this, your time and your talent, I thank you. It is a great honor to share the stage and these pages with your presence. Again, thank you to my readers. May this book grace your life and bless your relationships forever. Enjoy dears.

Thank you to Mr. Wil Brown, III, who was the one man that pushed me into purpose and made me understand the importance of pursuing my passion no matter what it cost! Thank you for being a great father to our children and being an arrow to help point them in the right direction! They are becoming all that we said that they would be.

Rest peacefully. Sunrise February 14, 1967, to Sunset July 09, 2011.

Love Is.......

Love is the one power that can transform all our lives. Love can create an environment that makes us come alive and be at ease. Love is a shelter from the rain of life. Love is past a feeling into purpose. Love leads and guides us into truth. Love covers all our human faults, frailties, and failures. Love outlasts anything and everything in life. Love does not know the grave; it remembers those who captured our hearts that no longer dwell here. Love is the master of meaning. Love is the passion that drives us to the arms of one another. Love is pure, purposeful, and painless. Love is the magic that reveals the meaning of why we choose one person over the other. Love is the perfect thing on earth. Love leads us to our purposed person and commands our undivided attention. Love arrest our hearts while captivating our minds. Love is the energy that wakes us up in the morning, and it is the same force that lays us peacefully to sleep at night. Love never fails. Love never changes. Love is consistent. Love is contagious. Love is captivating and calming. Love is beauty beyond one's body. Love is what we need to enjoy a perfectly imperfect person. Love is what brings a smile to our face while we dance away the night. Love is the laughter that we share while lying in each other's arms. Love is the exchange of spirit while connected to the soul of our commanded partner. We do not need love; we are LOVE because God created us, and He is LOVE. Love is EVERYTHING!

Welcome to "Why He Married Her & Played Me. Nine Secrets to What He's Thinking"

Introduction

Often in my journey through relational life, I find people that have had this not so exciting experience—being involved with someone from an intimate perspective only to find that you are not the only one. Not knowing that there is competition in the eyes of your man can be the ultimate wedge that drives you apart. "Why He Married Her & Played Me" is here to help you change all of that. Knowing these nine secrets to his decision can equip you with the information that you need so that you never get played again!

By playing, I mean that you will be aware of what is going on by the actions that he displays and not only the words that he speaks. No longer will you walk around with the relationship vail of trust covering your face. You will have the power to know the man that you are dealing with. There is nothing more powerful than being in the "know"!

As you read through these pages and learn from these amazing men, be sure to have your highlighters ready, honey, as there are some stellar messages that you do not want to forget!

This book is designed as a game-changer, truth bringer, and eye-opener! We will share tools with you that will not only stop the negative experience but enlighten, inspire, and educate you in your quest to identify your purposed person. Please join me as we take the journey to understand "Why He Married Her & Played Me, Nine Secrets to What He's Thinking" ......

Much love, peace, and respect to all the leading ladies! Coach Koffe

Coach P. Koffe Brown - Anthologist Visionary, CEO & Marketing Guru

What's the love of your life? For the speaker, certified life coach, and healing practitioner, P. Koffe Brown, it's empowering others to heal.

A proponent for living life with passion and purpose, Koffe's story is not much different from most of her clients. With astounding clarity borne from years of intensive work, Koffe has unraveled the impact of freedom in her life and recognized that her life's purpose revolves around supporting others in their journey to inner peace, wholeness, and love.

Koffe's combination of personal experience and professional skills compelled her to create *Destined for Greatness PAS* in 2003. Through inspirational speaking and coaching, Koffe takes clients on a transformational journey of healing and growth to incorporate a holistic approach to soul cleansing and deliberate change. She focuses on shifting relationship patterns, raising self-awareness, and channeling energies back to its true essence, one of divine spiritual love.

Driven by her mission to promote holistic growth, Koffe creates unique, powerful, and high energy experiences that delight others to take hold of their vision and put it into action. Embodying the essence of her core message, "Free your mind, and the past will soon be left behind!" Koffe contentedly fulfills her passion for serving others through coaching, writing, workshops, social media talk shows & live seminars.

An author, avid reader, lover of communication, and all things transformative, Koffe's mission is - and will forever be - to heal, inspire, and create change in the world, one heart at a time.

From the Poetic Genius herself, The Leading Lady

Coach P. Koffe Brown....

September 05, 2018

Dear Future, I mean, Dear NOW!

Not only am I grateful that you found me, but I am also thankful that I knew to **CHOOSE YOU**! See, we all have freedom of choice, and I admit my choices have not always been Divinely Orchestrated. My **FLESH** made my decisions in times past, which left me going in cycles, vicious ones at that. Before you came, I decided to **DIE** to the decisions that brought harm to me as a **WOMAN**. I could no longer live outside while bleeding to death internally. You see, your **ATTRACTION** to me was not just because of my bouncy booty, big breast, brown eyes, gracious smile, and the way I sashay your way. You saw the God in me, the oil from my being crushed into **PURITY**! You saw a **DIAMOND** who had gone through

FIRE to burn away all the filth from who I used to be. You saw a fighter who was not afraid to get in the ring and box with the enemy who wants to destroy humanity! You know you found me because it was time for **FAVOUR** to chase you down and you to be all that you could be for **GOD'S GLORY**! So, I choose you, a man after God's heart for me! People will be confused and dumbfounded when they find out that we walk together, equally yoked, and agree that no one or nothing comes before *God, the US, and our family*! I honor you, Sir, with my body, I respect your authority, and I stand beside you for as long as there is air in my lungs to breathe! Dear, **NOW** you have the absolute best of me!" *Signed a Queen Positioned,*

P. Koffe Brown

Honorable Mention Author
Dr. Adrian Woods EdD

Dr. Woods is a writer, poet, counselor, veteran, and educator. He holds five college degrees, including a Master's and Doctorate in education from the University of Houston Clearlake. He has a certification in counseling and mediation. Even with his credentials, he considers his most tremendous success as being a husband and father. He uses his experiences, both fantastic and tragic, to explore and articulate life mysteries to help others navigate through their trials and tribulations. In Adrian's downtime, he enjoys creating stellar content on his YouTube Channel and Collecting Invaluable Comic Books. Adrian is a SOLID guy!

Marriage Is Honorable

With
Dr. Adrian M. Woods

I have had the privilege of being married to the same beautiful woman for over twenty years. I will never forget the moment in 1995 when I first laid eyes on her. I have never really been a sentimental person, but at that moment, I knew love was real. Growing up, I never knew what a successful relationship looked like. I did not have a clue how to show this earth-bound angel the respect she deserved, but I knew I didn't want to spend one day without her. I made countless mistakes. I was a gang-banging street kid, and she was a pampered only child from the suburbs. Our entire viewpoints on life were different. There were times when I would be in the streets hustling, see that she blew up my pager with the code 9-1-1, and call to her in tears with worry. I could have lost her. I was more concerned with dealing dope than I was my future wife. It was during one of those conversations, with her in tears, that I realized that it was time to grow up. I had to learn the meaning of 1 Peter 3:7 and honor my future wife. But first, I had to figure out what "honoring her" meant.

According to Merriam-Webster's Dictionary, honorable means an action performed with high respect and guided by a keen sense of duty and ethical conduct. The word honorable is an adjective that has been used to describe several actions throughout human history. In ancient Japan, the samurai lived by a code of honor known as Bushido or the way of the warrior. This code of honor was not formally written down until the 17th century, but for centuries before, countless samurai devoted their lives to this code. The honor was held with such high regard that if one were to dishonor themselves or their families, they would sacrifice their lives in a ritualistic suicide called seppuku. These warriors devoted their entire existence to this way of life, to their land, their family, and their lord.

So devoted were these men that they would gladly lay down their lives. In the United States, the highest and most prestigious award given for an act of military service is titled the Medal of Honor. This award is only given to those military servicemen and women who set themselves apart from their peers through extreme acts of heroism and bravery. To be awarded the Medal of Honor, one must place their very life on the line to perform and act that goes above and beyond the call of duty. In the U.S. military's long history, only 3,506 individuals have earned this honor out of the countless men and women that have served our country.

As I continued to ponder the word honor and its meaning, I wondered when did the idea of marriage become less honorable. There should be no more tremendous honor than for one to devote their life to the one they love. We must remember that we are chosen. A man should feel a sense of honor that his wife chose him over countless suitors that pursued her. A woman should feel honored that she was the one her husband picked her to build his legacy with. They both should feel pride knowing that they have a soulmate to travel through life with, to laugh with, to raise kids with, to face adversity with, and hopefully go into glory with. When did the vows we take on our wedding day become negotiable? No longer is marriage "until death do us part," but more like "until I do not feel like dealing with you."

A marriage, in theory, is supposed to be a solemn promise to care for your life mate through all life's trials and tribulations. In modern times though, society often seems a victim of the fictitious Willie Lynch Letter, "How to Make a Slave." Man and woman have been pit against each other, believing they do not need each other. Men have been emasculated and seen as burdens that women have been forced to care for as if they were children. On the other hand, women are now taught not to depend on a man and to create their own. These beliefs are passed from mother to daughter and father to son, making generational curses that devalue the family dynamic.

Indeed, men and women do not need each other to survive. Both can work and provide themselves with nourishment and shelter, but I am not speaking of just staying. I am speaking of fulfilling your purpose. You need your spouse to complete God's plan for you. This is what the Bible means by being equally yoked. When the right two individuals bring their whole selves into a relationship, they can build and create a legacy. I promise you hard times will come. But when you are with that right person, you will have a partner to not only help you to make it through but will help you to rise to new heights. You will not have to worry about growing apart. Your lifemate will grow with you. Your partner will fight for you and pick you up when you fall.

Marriage is not a sprint. It is a marathon. The ring that each one wears on their left hand symbolizes that vow of eternal love. Marriages only fail when one person refuses to work. A man refuses to learn how to communicate, or a woman refuses to respect her husband. I have made it to twenty years of marriage because my wife is not an option. I work to honor her every day. Like the ancient samurai, the vows that we exchanged on our wedding day are my way of life. I wear my wedding band as a badge of honor. I see no more incredible benefit than pledging one's life to their spouse and walking through life hand in hand. So, all respect for those who choose us instead of me. The ones that choose to fight for their marriages when love seems all but lost. Those are the heroes. To those individuals go the honor.

Contributing Author
Jason Williams

Jason Williams is a preacher, businessman, and musician. He is a man that desires to reach every goal set before him. He is motivated in every area of his life using his gifts of speaking, music, and the stage to inspire and mentor people to grow by finding their true passion and potential.

CHAPTER 1

She Learned Me To Earn Me

With
Jason Williams

In every relationship, communication is critical, but I read a meme the other day that stated: "Communication is important, but Comprehension is most important." Often, when we get into a new relationship, we communicate, but we don't listen. We don't hear everything that's being said. We hear the parts that seem to excite us or move us, but we don't listen to the details that tell us who we're dealing with. What are their life experiences, what are their expectations? We don't always ask the most important questions because we assume it's too early, or maybe this isn't the right question to ask. Most of the real men I know will tell you we are who we are, and unless he is trying to be deceptive, what you see is what you get. When courting, if you aren't learning each other, then what's the point.

He needs to know all of you, and you need to know all of him. If he runs from questions, then he may have other issues, but at the same time, you need to be prepared to be asked questions you may not be comfortable answering also. Ultimately if you both are dating to make marriage the end, then no question is off-limit. Does he feel comfortable enough to talk to you about where he is without being belittled or feeling like your conversation will be in the next girl talk? Can he be vulnerable with you and not be looked at as soft or weak? Can he be truly open, and in heated discussions, it's not thrown back at him? Not negating your needs, but there has to be a level of reciprocity. He is picking her over you because she is giving him something you couldn't or wouldn't. If he is the one for you, then you need to hear his heart on his desires, his needs, and his wants.

Have you ever seen that couple that seems to be so opposite in appearance, and it's like what brought them together? Sometimes it's just the fact that they heard each other's hearts, and it caused a connection that can't be explained, but it is wholly felt when they are together.

We study to graduate school and to achieve most of the accomplishments in our lives but lack that same drive in relationships. If you learn each other with the intent to be everything the other needs, no one can get between you ever. Now, are there some anomalies, yes, but most people looking to get married looking to find that person that they will say compliments them. But what we should be looking for is the person that is willing to study them and know them at a level that answers their question by their actions, sometimes before the question is asked.

A relationship is a commitment to learning for the rest of your life if marriage is the end game.

You and he both should show signs by actions that during the conversation, you heard each other and are taking steps to prove that. What we learn should, in most cases, lead to some action that shows we learned and adapted. But once again, this is reciprocal. One side should not be proving there is understanding without the other showing the same. You both need to learn the deal-breakers—the ones that are said and those that are not. I don't believe they are the same for every man, but most men agree with these few.

For starters, no man wants a woman that's been with everybody. No man wants to feel like there are men that can tell you about your lady or especially your wife. Two, no man wants to be disrespected privately or publicly. Not being able to have control of your emotions can only create more frustrations. Three. No man wants to feel he is not needed. If every time you need help, you have another source, or he isn't your first choice, then what is he there for? Even if he can't do what is necessary, at least give him the first right of refusal. Then he knows you are looking for him to be that man for you and that you value his ability to do or just his input. But he also needs to learn your deal breakers, spoken and unspoken. Every relationship has its language and not the five love languages, but how the couple interacts with each other. You both have to figure out each other enough to understand the language of your relationship. Your language means the way you both communicate with each other. The spoken and the unspoken things that make your language unique. Your language is as individual as your fingerprint. The way you speak to each other, the way you read each other's body language, the way you respond to confrontation. Others may see your relationship as odd, but if it works for you, then it works for you. Loving anyone requires a continuous educational process. You have to be willing to be forever in school and committed to the process.

You have to understand people do change, and many things will be different as we age. So are you willing to be pliable enough to give grace through the periods of growth that will come later? Are you ready to give grace in areas that may even challenge your norms as long as they are not deal breakers? Do you know the career goals of your significant other? Do you know where they want to be in five or ten years in business?

Not only do you need to know what their goals are, but can you support them along their journey. Are you willing to fight for their dream as if it were your own? Can you help them if it creates some financial hardship without destroying their vision of their professional progress? Are you willing to learn the way your companion likes to spend their down or free time? Are they a homebody, or are they the type that wants to be out and about?

Are they people or group-oriented, or do they prefer to be in just your presence? And are you able to accept how they choose to spend their free time even if you are the opposite?

Now, don't get me wrong there should always be some compromise, but if you feel like it's not your mode of thinking for your time, can you deal with doing some things on your own without feeling a sense of disconnect or alienation from your significant other? Do you know what their idea of what family looks like? How many kids, if any? How they choose to parent?

Are you willing to compromise if it doesn't match your idea of family? Do you know of any possible existing medical conditions that may come up later that can affect your life? Do they have any family history with addictions that, if not checked, could creep into your relationship? There are so many questions that need to be explored, but ultimately you both need to be utterly and completely honest to every question.

Don't choose not to speak on a subject just because you feel it's unimportant right now, or right now, it doesn't matter. Neither hides something because you don't want to feel judged or ridiculed for being different. You both should be authentically you so that you both know precisely what you are walking into with no secrets or hidden agendas.

Change is inevitable for both parties, and both have to accept the fact that change is the most constant thing that they will experience, and being able to adjust will help at every stage of evolution. Each individual needs to learn enough to be able to acknowledge their strengths and weaknesses. HEAR ME.... ACKNOWLEDGE YOUR STRENGTHS AND YOUR WEAKNESSES.

There are plenty of people that know what their strengths and weaknesses are but don't acknowledge them in the proper perspectives. So, you both need to be able to accept the strengths and weaknesses as if they will never change.

Not assuming weaknesses will change. You will love them out of it, because you may never see that come to fruition. Is either of you willing to accept the things you can't stand about the other without expecting change? Not looking to mold them or push them out of that particular character flaw. Both have to learn to accept even when others say, "I wouldn't take that, as long as you." That's what you are willing to accept.

As I stated earlier, every relationship has its language. If you both interact, it is suitable for both of you. If you both are delighted, then don't compare your significant other or your relationship to any other. Don't allow what others project to dictate what you do or how you do because, in the end, you two have to live with the consequences of your reality.

Form what I call your circle as a couple. Don't allow anything or anyone to infiltrate your circle with something that both of you haven't agreed together on.

Your circle is your sanctuary and place of peace. Nothing should come in and destroy your tranquility as a couple. This has to be created from what you both have learned from each other and what is accepted by each other. Your circle is your place of agreement on the things you all have peace about. The position of acceptance between you both and the understanding that you both are good. You both should be each other's peace, safe place, and shoulder to lean on. You both should be the first person you want to talk to when something good or bad comes up.

A lot of women may not realize that the woman you are can help to push your man to be the best version of himself. How you ask? When he feels you love him unconditionally and that you are with him and for him. He needs to know he is not your financier, not daddy to your kids, not something of convenience or anything outside of being your companion.

All the other stuff is great, and he will freely be when he feels you want him and the best for him. Now I am sure some of you are saying, "yeah, right, I did all of that." Don't get me wrong; there are males out there that have not entirely matured and want to play the games. But when he is ready and genuinely concerned about his future and family, he will see your efforts and won't let you give out real love without reciprocating it. You learning him will make him know you and all the things it takes to make you smile outside of the bedroom. Most men that want to be married are not looking for their mother, a maid, baby incubator, or just a roommate with benefits. He wants the woman that is ready to know him and be his complete companion.

Now I know the title of this chapter is "She Learned me to Earn me," but I believe if you were paying attention, you see both have to commit to learning each other. There should never be a time in your relationship that you are not learning the nuances of the one you say you love.

Neither of you can do it alone. Both parties have to be fully invested in time and effort to learn if you can make it. The bible says, "my people perish for the lack of knowledge....," That applies to every area of your life. Wherever you lack understanding, you may let something fall through the cracks and not even notice it because you are completely unaware that something is wrong. There is no magic potion or secret algorithm to make relationships work.

Each relationship is different, just like each individual. You both have to make time to study each other to reach a great relationship. Most people visualize a relationship as a trip going from A to B in a straight line. That is not how it works; it's a more like spiraling between A and B. Sometimes, you are moving forward; sometimes, you are moving backward. But if you are learning, every move forward is larger than any step back, which keeps you moving in the right direction.

You have to applaud the forward moments and learn from the back steps to not have to repeat steps. Anything worth having doesn't come easy, and anything that comes easy most times is not worth having.

Contributing Author
Danai Young

Danai was born in Fresno, CA. Where his remarkable natural athletic abilities developed. The love of sports led Danai to the University of Nebraska at Lincoln, where he earned a bachelor's degree in Sociology and Psychology. Upon graduating, Mr. Young was afforded a 14-year professional international basketball career where he played in 13 different countries. Currently, he resides in Las Vegas, Nevada, where he crafts the art of writing and motivational speaking. Mr. Young is an advocate for healthy families and prides himself on being a Leader for all who dream big. Danai's philosophy is, "Anything is possible with God by your side." He also believes, "If God is not a part of it, it won't work, nor will it last."

CHAPTER 2

You Never Gave Him A Reason To Commit

With
Danai Young

So, you've made it here. What do I mean by that? You still have this book in your hand, hopefully in search of some inspiration and guided correction. I Promise I will not short change you, so let's keep it honest here.

Maybe, just maybe, your failed relationship(s) had less to do with him and so much more to do with you. Big sigh, let it out, I encourage you to. I'm going to break it down in this chapter in a few different scenarios. At the end of each scenario, we will arrive at a critical point that you may apply and use in your growth, correction, and, best of all, your next fulfilling relationship.

Take your time taking this all in. Most importantly, be real with yourself about how you represent yourself as a woman and what you truly want for your future.

Let's Dive In!

You Were Not Healed

With a broken heart, you were not ready for him. You forced yourself to get in the streets instead of sitting your ass down somewhere. You set yourself up for failure from the jump. You see, he did not know the extent of your pain. He did not think you were not prepared to be a wife. He spent more time trying to patch up wounds from your past, that he couldn't explore the real you and your healed heart. You thought he wouldn't notice how easily you triggered, taking out your aggressions on him, traces of what your last partner did to you.

See, if you had taken the time and invested in your recovery, you would have been able to have a healed, refreshed heart to present and give him. Yet you came in broken, and he was healed, causing him to rethink his plans with you. And let me tell you this, it was easy for him to leave because a healed man can't fix a broken woman. Queen, healing is your responsibility alone.

Key Points

"There is purpose in unconditional healing… A healed heart allows you to Love someone with Freedom and Peace!"

You Wanted to Build A Man

Let's get this out of the way first, a perfect man does not exist, but you are not trying to hear that. You thought you could mold a man into what you wanted him to be. How he acts, how he talks, what he eats, wears, etc…… I'm sure you get the picture. You cared more about what you thought he needed to do instead of what he wanted to do.

Just as fast as you were trying to build him, you were tearing him down at the same time with your demands. It was easy for him to chuck you the peace sign; you made him feel like a prisoner of love, instead of a man in love. And on top of that, you had the nerve to get mad at him because he left; you looked at him as an investment and not your Man. Can you blame him for leaving?

Key Points

"This is not Build-A-Bear, and the man in your life should not be your robot."

Understand two is better than one and compromised compatibility never produces favor.

Teamwork will make the dream work!!!

You Never Left the Nest

So, you want your family in all the business, huh? You're more committed to your family than the relationship. He competed with your family; he walked on eggshells around your family. The family had way too much dictatorship in your relationship. You rarely heard him when he voiced his opinion about the situation. Every time he spoke his piece about it, you attacked him, kept telling him he did not like your family reversing the role of concern to guilt. Always throwing in his face how much more your family meant to you than the relationship.

You often played both sides and kept up the mess; he heard from your family over and over that he was not a good fit for you. It should not matter who your Man is in front of or around; family included, if you genuinely care about him, he should always feel confident and comfortable in your company and space.

There is no reason for him to feel less than. He should always feel like a Man, and your family should know you are rocking with him heavily. You are a representation of one another. But because you never left the nest, he left you. He was left feeling like a victim instead of your companion. The blessing was walking away for him.

Key Points

"Never let your family dictate the commitment to the Man you say you love and are rocking with. He deserves his own nest and your best!"

He Was Looking for A Wife, Yet You Were A Girlfriend

Many times, so many women swear they are wife material, when their entire vibe says, "I'm just a girlfriend." I'm saying it is written all over their face, from their actions down to the words that come out their mouths.

A man that is genuinely in search of a wife sees himself as a husband in his singleness. He is not trying to waste time with a girl who is acting without readiness but would instead continue to search for a woman who knows and is committed to preparing her life to be in a healthy relationship leading up to marriage, no acting required. And let's not get it twisted; actions don't make you a wife, sex doesn't make you a wife, having babies don't make you one either.

Your beliefs, your soul, your understanding, your healing, and most importantly, your relationship with The Most High lend you the capability of being a good wife and lifelong partner, The Virtuous Wife! Queen, you have got to drop the "fake it to you make it" act. And stop treating your boyfriend like a husband. And know this, a man knows when he has found his wife, and he will let it be known.

Key Points

"Be a wife in your singleness, so when your husband comes, you'll recognize him, and you will be prepared!"

You Didn't Know What You Wanted

Confused about it all, the past, the present, and the future?? Yet you want to question the Man about his position in your life. He is just as confused as you are. Every time he asks a question, you don't know. You have settled so much in life that you have no idea he wanted you as his wife. Too caught up in past relationships! Also concerned about his past relationships!

Never genuinely paying attention to his pure motive for you and would have been a blooming relationship. He wanted to move forward, but just couldn't because you were stuck in the "I Don't Know," and knew what he did and didn't want. No one puts on their checklist an indecisive woman, please.

Key Points

"Queen, when you are writing your checklist of what you want in a man, make sure you are also writing down what you don't want. Make it clear, and I promise to find love won't be as hard. You'll truly eliminate wasted time. Stop letting people play with you and stop playing yourself.

There is purpose in knowing what you do and don't want!"

Financial Corruption

Now I have saved the best for last because really, this topic here is a 2-edge sword. When it comes to finances, I am a firm believer that two is better. But I'm no fool to what this world believes and what I have personally experienced. What the world tells women is that if his bank account is not deserving, neither is he. And you're eating that up, looking past if he is a good man, good father, loves God, and loves himself. Queen, your need for financial stability scared him because your expectation was "You Got Me." You put it all on him. Buy this, buy that. You have a worthy man and him explaining to you that saving is best; you never know what the future may bring is responsible and honorable. But you were not trying to hear that. You made it clear that if he couldn't provide, you were stepping, so he stepped before it could even come to that. Your financial demands were his walking papers.

Key Points

Financial Communication is Key… "Queens understand that it's no longer just yours. You have to look for more in a man than just a financial provider. Know that husbands provide not only finances but unconditional prayer, love, peace, happiness, and laughter!"

The Mirror

Accountability has so much purpose to it. Take a look in the Mirror. What do you see? Let's take this time to reflect. Did any of those scenarios fit who you are today or who you used to be? If it's the latter and you have moved passed this, Congratulations! You have successfully matured and blossomed and are possibly ready to engage in a fantastic successful long-term relationship with the right Man.

If you are just not there yet, it's ok. The first step to changing any behavior is acknowledgment. To you, I say this; correction is renewing. You have made it this far. To further your growth, I ask that you revisit this chapter and implement the critical points in your life. Know this; the Mirror will tell you a lot about yourself. Dig deep into your soul and find the real you.

Permit yourself to pour lots of love into you for the healing you so deserve, and God wants you to have. Do not forget to create your list of dos and don'ts and refine it as you grow. You're so worth it. My very last take away is for you always to remember that the best you is the authentic one, strip out and shed all of the baggage and let him see your glow.

Contributing Author
Charles Dixon III

Charles Dixon III is determined to challenge the way people think about love and relationships. He is an Inspirational Speaker based in Chicago. In 2017 he began his public speaking career when he participated in a platform discussion for men on the topic of relationships. This fueled his passion and inspired him to start his first "live" radio show in 2017.

He has been on a mission of *"healing the world, one heart at a time"* ever since. His show, "Unique Perspectives Love Talk Radio®," is a reasoning platform created to spark dialogue about the challenges of relationships and dating today. Charles is bold and brings unconventional and controversial topics to the conversation, which has been the basis for many of his subsidiary shows.

Charles is CEO of Charles Dixon IP, Intellectual Property Portfolio Management®. Charles loves people and aims to help them reach their potential, dreams, goals, and inspirations. He is a certified life coach at his business, A Bridge Over Life Coaching Services®.

He is also a gifted singer, songwriter, and recording artist under the name *Da Liberal Soul*® with over 8 recorded albums. For fun, he also enjoys transforming personal spaces into classic life-long conversation pieces for his side business Unique Eyes Contemporary Furnishings & Designs®.

CHAPTER 3

You're A Placeholder, Not A Partner

With
Charles Dixon III

Wait... wait... wait! Before we get started, hold on to your wig, weave, or hat as I am about to help you understand the "ugly" truth about the Placeholder/Partner scenario. Men are fully aware of with whom they would like to spend their time and with whom they want to build a future (i.e., that is, opposed to the woman with whom he undoubtedly knows he's just wasting time). This internal debate is a futile exercise, more than anything because, as men, we are not created to exist in the gray when it comes to love. Either we see the vision at first "hello" from the one we can potentially see as our "partner," or conversely, we accept the situational real estate from the "placeholder," the one we relegate to "between the sheets" tenants (or occupiers). Unfortunately, it can be no other way, or it would go against nature for him as he was created as a visionary. If it were any other way, a man would be incapable of being the head of his family and would lack the ability to lead.

Let's be clear; there is a distinct difference between "building with a partner" and existing with "interim booty" (i.e., the Placeholder). For example, spending time and making plans are associated with building something more permanent and stable, whereas getting the proverbial 'booty' is associated with lies and deceit. If you subscribe to the modern-day narrative that some men peddle, you may be operating, unknowingly, under the guise of 'openness, truth, and honesty,' otherwise known as "hiding in plain sight," when, in fact, you're really "on hold." Under this guise, you will feel warm and fuzzy upfront and may even feel you're respected; however, you are, nonetheless, his "on hold" hostage.

There are many intricate parts to a man. In many cases, from the hurt we have experienced in our past relationships, there are many layers to be unfolded before we can come to the place of being ready for that life partner. For instance, a man will do many hurtful and questionable things while building with his life partner. However, in his mind, all the insanity and pain are necessary parts of the process for him to make with her. Sounds crazy, right? Sadly, it's true.

Think of a tree where some of the protruding branches can wound you if you brush against them. Nevertheless, as thorny and rough as the branches may appear, the tree is still growing, still vulnerable. Such is the case with a man who is still building in the trenches of his life. The question is, can his forever partner handle his growth process? Most would think that because a man makes a left turn and does things contrary to the building process with his partner, his trajectory has changed, when, in reality, it has not. He still desires to keep moving forward and sincerely wants to get it right. How often have you heard the saying, "He needs to grow up"?

Well, to tell a man to grow up means that he needs to grow out of something, which can be very uncomfortable for him and the woman in his life. For a man to really "grow up," he most likely will have to grow to a place where he is wiser and less selfish. He would have to grow into space, mentally, where his focus has shifted from conquering and straying to focusing and staying. Men are continually evolving, which can be challenging, but for a man to be deemed as a "good" man, he will learn through trials and tribulations to build character. It is an ugly road, but it is the journey that will help develop his character and prepare him for his life partner. Until a man reaches that level of self- awareness and wisdom, he orchestrates the PLIGHT OF

THE PLACEHOLDER...the "booty."

The immense nuance in the world of "placeholding" is the selfishness when it comes to the Placeholder.

There is an unspoken question that you are asking a person, and that is, "please wait with me until SHE comes?" Let's break down this word "placeholder," as it pertains to relationships -- the "place" is where he aspires to be, and the "holder" is his selfish reality. The role of a placeholder, from my perspective, can be compared to a place setting. A place setting is simply the position or act of occupying a space, which is what a placeholder does in the life of a man that only views a woman in the "now" (the playmate) and never the "permanent" (the life partner). The "placeholder" often serves the purpose of love-readiness for a man. She allows him to practice being in a relationship without requiring him to commit. The most significant premise about a "placeholder" is

DENIAL, which is where THE PURPOSE OF THE PLACEHOLDER erects (uhmm…pun intended).

When a man allows a woman "access," it often makes the woman believe "I AM HIS WOMAN."

She will also think about the carbon copy commitment he provides, causing the "placeholder" to think that she is in a relationship. When a man sees a woman only when it is convenient for him, and she is granted overnight visits only, with no quality time, the primary form of communication is by text message.

The promises never come to fruition; these restrictions are placed on the 'placeholder" because he is waiting on the partner he deems the "ONE." On the flip side, the woman he sees as his life partner can also become a placeholder if he married her. Still, she wasn't the "one." It's all a matter of his perspective and what he needs for that moment versus what he sees for his future.

It doesn't matter how cute you think you are, how many coins are in your bank account, how thin or fluffy you are, or how genuine you maybe if a man deems you as the "placeholder," that is, simply who you will be to him. "Placeholders" don't move off the shelf, except to get rearranged. There is no progression, no shift in position; you are there to serve the purpose as the "prop," not used in "real-time."

One of the traits of the "placeholder" is that she resembles his best friend. There is no risk associated with her, so it's easy for him to have access to her, which is why he may stay longer than he originally intended. The selfish part of it all is that the minute you allow him to "practice" with you, you become a still-figment of his imagination while he continues to search for his right partner, while in some cases, the life partner is already there. It's unfortunate, but it's the "ugly" truth of many men.

Then there are times, where a woman will label herself as the partner and write out the entire script of the relationship in her mind when in reality, he's not that interested in her and never had any real intent to make her his wife.

The liability comes into play when she chooses to be patient, assuming she can convert his disinterest into interest. This responsibility solely falls on her for staying even if she claims he led her on. If we are honest, we all know that exciting feeling when our name or number is called when it's our turn, and we also know the loathsome feeling of sitting forever in the waiting room. Therefore, you should practice doing what feels right to your heart and stop settling for someone who will not completely commit to you.

A woman was not designed to build muscle in the gym of love, so if you find yourself doing the heavy lifting and pursuing, you are likely attached to the wrong trainer (i.e., the wrong man). The bottom line is if you are chasing him, and he is not buying what you're selling, he will stay, play, and bide his time until he finds the "one."

Ok, Placeholder, here's a word directly to you. When we think about accountability and the Placeholder and why the "job" prerequisite was created, it's because you likely dressed for the part. What do I mean? Today, with the many social media platforms and peer pressure, many women adorn themselves to "look" the part and be all things external for the "catch."

When you catch a man based off on your outward appearance, he probably sees you as "shallow" and will likely continue his search for his "real" partner. Men "fall" for the "deep," but they sleep in the shallow end of the pool. In other words, the more substance you show, the less likely you are to be put on "hold." You will either come dressed to sit like a "placeholder," or you will come dressed to stand and walk with him like his "partner."

Your presentation says it all. Yes, it is true, we men judge from the door. It's sad, but it's an ugly truth.

Taking a deeper dive into the presentation piece and how the "external" has been the hook and bait for many men, and truthfully, has been our demise, has caused more grief than we are prepared to handle. Let's face it, too much of anything can't be too good for anyone. If a woman is only good as far as the eye can see, it will eventually become a strain because the very thing that we like to parade can be the same thing that we become insecure about.

If she's only suitable for a certified arm piece (i.e., a dime-piece), depending on the type of person she is, that could be a lot of baggage. Therefore, we need to get out of the business of "mousetrapping" and get into the habit of "house-preparing." A wise woman knows the real answer to her destiny is really how well she prepares her house; it's not just the external; it's EVERYTHING!

When a woman is house-preparing, that man comes in, and he grows from it, and he invites others to witness his peace and pleasure.

However, women who subscribe to thinking about their appearance and outgoing personality alone will hook a man, risk becoming repetitive and repellant. She is merely laying a bunch of "cheese" to catch him, but when she captures him, she does not know what to do with him in his entirety. Think about it, a mousetrap is meant for death, and the mouse that doesn't die is wounded, is in danger, and is never the same.

If we give more thought to this idea of placeholding, another underlying feature of the Placeholder is birthed when a man realizes this is someone, he has feelings for, cares a lot about, and in some cases may even love, but knows for sure she is not someone who matches his ideal future. She, as in the "placeholder," might align with him sexually, financially, or even emotionally in some cases, but it does not mean she connects with the rest of his life's necessities.

The reasons for the conflict of interest could be several things; however, the REAL REASON is the issue of IMAGE and the stress to obtain and maintain the perfect picture of it. A man defines a woman one of two ways, as it pertains to his partner if that's what he's seeking: the shortfall vs. the long haul. He knows he can fall intimately with them both, but he wants to fall endlessly in an all-encompassing version of love. It also comes down to who he believes he can endure life with and the one he feels can weather all seasons of him, and once he realizes HER, he puts into play the PLAN OF EXIT FOR THE PLACEHOLDER.

Just like your company's evacuation plan, a man almost always knows where every exit point is located within the relationship. Therefore, when the exit occurs, it feels abrupt and gut-wrenching to the recipient, but it's certainly not new news to him, whereas the man already had the blueprint laid out.

I'm sure no one wants to be in a person's holding cell, but many times it has to do with how you've positioned yourself. The whole exit process can be a short or a long-drawn-out battle where the environment is much like one's "Miranda Rights," where everything you say can and will be critically used against you as a weeding tool to prove or support his case for exiting, or for her reasoning as to why it shouldn't be over. No matter the fight, the exit is inevitable because his heart has already grasped his future, and grasping his end is his motivation for DISINFECTING FROM THE PLACEHOLDER.

Before you get upset, let me explain. The process of disinfecting from the Placeholder means to disengage, cleanse your mindset, and focus on the fact that you are whole, you are enough, and your partner is worth it. It comes down to a choice that must be made. The process is critical to the survival and the success of the relationship with your partner.

Why? When we, as men, find ourselves in need of someone to be in a holding place in our lives, we are indeed acknowledging that we are crippled and need a crutch. To sum it up, that's indeed what the Placeholder is, the crutch until you can walk with that life partner. In other words, men, if you need a placeholder, you probably don't need to be married. So, ladies, who may consider yourselves "the partner" or "partner material," you still need to carry a certain level of concern as to whether the man that's asking you to be his wife is indeed ready. If he remains disabled or maimed, at some point, he will be unmotivated to evolve away from that crutch (i.e., he's going to continue requiring that crutch). He will need another handler and will eventually require them to sit with him while he lives with you, thus creating another placeholder.

Furthermore, men may even place a crazy woman on hold. Her craziness doesn't phase him because he likely already had her in the cage called "his box." Therefore, men

can weave in and out of several personality types because his intention is not to move her along, but it's to study her while she's still. Some placeholders try to make sense of who they are, their position, even as placeholders, because technically, he's right in the box with her until he decides to give up residency in that box when he recognizes and acknowledges his life partner.

I know you're thinking, if he's held up in the box with me, how does he make it to her, his life partner? Simple, let's remember you're standing still, while he is always moving and being the organically bred hunter that he was born to be. Men are straightforward and concise creatures; they know when to play, and they know when they are expected to get brave. The problem is, depending on the example he was shown in his early years as a boy, the women he chooses will often experience more of the boy in him, with childish behavior, than the man version of him.

This is how he can have a lifetime of women in the holding pattern called the "placeholder" because he is still in a state of a yet born male (i.e., "baby boy"). To a man, a partner is a woman where he can see her purpose within his business plan, called his life, as it relates to the union of marriage.

There are a lot of women who are positioned in someone's waiting room that have already missed their name being called due to being at the wrong place with the wrong person at the wrong time, when in fact, you are genuinely someone else's absolute dream. The lesson is not to allow yourself to be auctioned off as unclaimed freight when someone else is waiting for their soulmate to arrive, they are waiting for you. Do not waste time where you are not appreciated. If your very presence does not motivate him to move on your behalf, nothing else will.

As for the partner, the partner is one who brings solidarity to his world. This is the very thing that grounds and settles a man in his spirit.

Before connecting with his partner, the unrest he experiences in his life causes him to foster "placeholder" relationships due to him being out of sync with his spirit. Much like the wall outlet that delivers power, a man desires to connect to his life's purpose and life partner. The life partner doesn't have to be perfect; she has to be enough for him. To add a little real-time context to this topic, for many years, I operated in this space and concept of thinking.

I felt it was important to always align myself with either the purpose-driven person, the partner-hopeful, or the purpose-like person, the Placeholder. So, I know firsthand that no one wins using this type of logic.

She gets held back and led on, and you restrict your happiness. She wants you, but you see her differently because you envision yourself with another. Either way, it's a miserable existence. She's beholden, and you are always left dreaming of another place.

To put a cap on that unscrupulous way of surviving, I had to realize that the person on hold was ME! I refused to give real love a chance. I was fighting my internal thoughts and fears of being loved unconditionally, despite my flaws. I had to release the fear of judgment and liberate myself to love and be loved in its full totality so that I can honestly say what is right or wrong in the land of love.

Stay tuned; my story isn't over…This is only the beginning!

Contributing Author
Kent Williams

Kent Williams is an author, life/relationship coach, businessman, and experienced IT professional. He has created and grown several network marketing businesses. He is a recent co-host on an online radio show featured segment, "HE says, SHE says," which deals with various topics and challenging aspects of relationships that men and women face every day. Kent is also a member of an all-male panel consisting of six men called the "THE MALE PERSPECTIVE" who give a Christian, male point of view to the many dating challenges that men face today

Kent's primary passion is to empower men and women to build more robust family units by cultivating better relationships through counseling, media, and books/eBooks. Kent has experienced many ups and downs throughout his life, but the one thing that drives him is his strong belief in God. It is this belief that propels him through the pitfalls and valleys we call life. He is currently building a Life Coaching Business, which will consist of webinars/seminars, workshops, 1-on-1 coaching, and books focused on helping individuals gain a new perspective. Kent's objective is to help people have healthier relationships by empowering them with the skills to better connect with the people in their lives one person at a time, one family at a time, all the while helping them find their real purpose in life that God has called them to fulfill.

CHAPTER 4

You Were Not Marriage Material

With
Kent Williams

What does it mean not to be "Marriage Material"? It can be a variety of issues that disqualify a woman from being marriage material, from a woman not dealing with the problems stemming from not having a father in her life to evaluating every man she comes in contact with from a superficial standpoint to being conditioned by Society on being so independent that the man doesn't know what his part in the relationship is. And there's a host of other derivatives that can come into play with this common issue. In this chapter, we will dive in-depth into what it means to be or not be marriage material.

YOU HAVEN'T HEALED YET

This is probably the most common issue on whether a woman is marriage material or not. Speaking from experiences of some of the women I've dealt with, it isn't easy to try and build a stable relationship with someone who is emotionally scarred. Trust issues, feelings of abandonment, and jealousy are just some of the obstacles one may have to conquer in dealing with a person who hasn't healed from issues from their past. The very first step to qualifying as a possible mate for a worthy man is first to realize that you are the problem, then take the time and steps needed to heal from these past issues.

Any man that knows his value doesn't require a whole lot of time to realize if the woman he is dating is marriage material or if she is going to end up being a side chick. If it's been six months to a year and you haven't met any of his family (especially his mom), or whenever he talks about the future, "he" is all that is mentioned instead of "we," then chances are good that you're not the one.

When a woman breaks up from a relationship, some physical and emotional ties need to be broken and dissolved. Sometimes a person can go about the healing process on their terms with no real outside help other than conferring with close friends and family. However, there are times where a woman may need professional help, amongst additional support to help her get past the difficulties of moving on from that past relationship. With whatever path that woman needs to take, there has to be ample time for healing to take place for her to be at peace and comfortable with herself. Otherwise, the relationship she enters in will be doomed to fail, and sometimes with dire consequences.

There was one woman I dated one summer that really could not get out of her way. She seemed like a nice person at first, and we had a lot of mutual interests, including football. But as I got to know her and her past, I found out that she was the victim of a lot of abuse-emotionally and physically.

Furthermore, she did not know her father, so right away, that were some serious red flags that I encountered. Then I noticed the trust issues she had. She was always suspicious if I was talking to someone, and she was very argumentative and high strung. This relationship was pretty much over before it ever began.

Nevertheless, whether it is spending some quality with close friends or family members, enjoying a spa day to pamper herself, to take a course online on a subject, she always wanted to learn a woman needs to broaden her horizons and stretch her boundaries farther than she ever has before. This can give her a high sense of accomplishment that heals the soul and gives her more confidence in every other aspect of her life, which in turn will essentially make her that much more attractive to the right man in her life.

TOO SUPERFICIAL

Now I believe every woman is beautiful in her own right. However, in Society, we have been conditioned to idolize physical beauty alone. If you don't have exceptional beauty, especially in the world of media or entertainment or loads of money, you're pretty much considered a nobody. We are visual creatures, and nowhere is that more apparent than with men. Now women of today know this all too well, and many of them will not hesitate to use that to their advantage. Now that's not saying it's a bad thing to want to look your best when you go out on a date. However, too many women these days are defined by their beauty and not enough by their substance. In other words, their physical beauty outweighs what inner beauty they have.

There was this Haitian girl I dated back in my teenage years that was very pretty naturally, but for whatever reason, maybe insecurity issues, she would lay it on thick with the makeup. I told her from time to time that she didn't need that much makeup on her face because she had naturally beautiful features that did not need to be enhanced. But it seemed like it went in one ear and out the other. For her and a lot of other girls in the area, there was a lot of pressure to be at peak beauty. But if there is no inner foundation or core moral values for that beauty to lean on, then you're just going to blend in with all the rest of the females that are vying for that good man. Because I don't care how on point you make yourself, whether you have a stride like a model or have a body like a Coke bottle. There will always be another female that will outdo you.

There always is constant competition with the woman in this world as to who is the prettiest or sexiest bombshell in any given place, and we as men play it to the fullest. Yet we know deep down that we will never marry most of the women we see in the streets, clubs, etc. because most of the females we come across are basically for show and tell.

They have no real internal value to them, and as I mentioned earlier in this chapter, we don't need much time before we can decipher which category that woman will fall under. It may seem that way for some women because most of the men that they have dealt with seem always to be dragging their feet at the thought of matrimony. But when we have it in our minds that this person is "The One," you will see a whole different type of man from the one who drags his feet to the kind of man who initiates and gets things done as only a true man is capable of doing.

Too many women today fail to realize that to be considered marriage material, it's not about the outer appearance but the inner beauty that flows from within. The confidence in how she walks, talks, and carries herself so that any man, whether he's worthy of her or not, notices instantly. With a woman like this, it will not take long to seal the deal. Trust me.

Women need to realize what image or vibe they give off whenever they focus too much on their outer appearance. No man, no matter how desirable he may find you, will ever respect and value you if he views you as just a trophy or a side chick. Yet, I have seen many a woman fails miserably because she thought she was "Mrs. Right" when all the while, he saw her as "Ms. Right Now." Now that's not to say enhancing your looks is a bad thing in general, as long as it's not the primary focus. High-value women don't have to rely solely on outward appearance to attract a man, as they know that their real beauty flows from within. What women should strive for is the right balance of building up their inner selves while enhancing their outer appearance.

We, like people, cannot feed into what Society deems is beautiful. Every woman has a hidden beauty about her that, under the right circumstances, can shine just bright as the rising sun. When a woman is genuinely connected to their purpose and secure in who they indeed are as a person,

not to mention having a strong spiritual connection with God or higher being, then that is when the true essence of that person comes out, which makes the person all the more beautiful no matter what their outer shell looks like.

THE INDEPENDENT WOMAN

This will probably be my most controversial topic in this whole chapter. However, it is because of this particular subject that I tuned in on a radio show segment some years ago. It is what sparked this journey of my passion for relationships between men and women. It happened about ten years ago while I was in Atlanta. One Sunday night on my way home from work, I happened to tune in on one of my favorite radio stations, only to find they weren't playing any music; instead, they were doing a radio segment which highlighted why independent, successful women, particularly in the Atlanta area are still single. While I admit I never thought about the subject until then, as I listened intently, I started thinking of all the successful women I know. And as you may have guessed, most of them were just that, single.

I was so intrigued by the segment I stayed in the car until the part was over, which must have been at least an hour. From that moment on, I looked at this topic differently and started writing my take on the subject and even conducting my interviews either by phone or in-person with many women I know to get their opinion on the topic. I learned quite a bit from their input as to why women who are independent and successful remain without a partner. According to some, it was their choice, but for others, it was circumstantial. For the sake of this chapter, we will focus more on the latter. About why some women are not **"Marriage Material."**

What I got out of the segment is that there is an increasingly growing number of successful women who cannot find a partner that fits their needs, and many of them that were interviewed were perplexed to why they couldn't find a good man. Were there standards too high? Were they giving off the wrong vibes to the right men? Or a host of other possible scenarios.

So, let's dive into how Society has conditioned the independent woman to be the man instead of keeping a man. As we all know, women have made their presence known in the workplace and corporate America, and deservingly so. All of their accomplishments and degrees are to be honored and respected without a doubt. But the truth of the matter is when it comes to attraction or marriage, a woman's accomplishments are usually not first on a man's list. Sure, he may find it attractive that the woman he's with has a degree or is the CEO of her company, but unless the man is looking for a come up, that's usually not the deciding factor of whether he wants to marry her or not.

Why do you see a rich guy end up with a girl that's a bartender or someone that works in fast food? Not saying that's precisely going to be a recipe for success, but men are more attracted to appearance because we are visual creatures. Then we want to know if a woman can hold us down and provide emotional support, especially during tough times. During the times of strife, a man looks to a woman who holds him up emotionally the most, not necessarily someone who has the degree or the high paying job, and of course, she has to be a good cook like mom used to be.

An Independent Woman these days can not only bring home the bacon; but can also get the whole pig and cook it too. For a long time now, women have been conditioned to be healthy and aggressive, whether it be at home or mainly in the workforce, which may be necessary for that respect. But when it comes to relationships and marriage, a woman and man should strive for Interdependence, in other words. In this relationship, both people rely on each other instead of just themselves to fulfill their needs. In today's world, women are often viewed as being self-reliant; however, too much of that can kill a relationship because the man has no idea where he fits into this situation.

If a man has no purpose or doesn't understand what his role in the relationship is, he more often than not will fail to fulfill the needs of his mate; and will likely find someone else that gives him a sense of purpose and makes him feel like the man he is. If a woman finds a way to switch from the independence mindset when it comes to dating or relationships, it has a good chance of improving substantially. It's all about letting him have a role in the relationship, even if she has all the answers. This also helps in her evaluation of her mate for three main reasons:

1. It lets him know that he is needed

2. Shows how committed he is to her and the relationship

3. Invites a sense of security for her that she can rely on him when she needs him most

All the while, this increases the bond between the two of them, making it stronger. Plus, it enables the man to do what he is programmed best to do: provide and protect his lady. If this is not nurtured during the dating stages, then men are not going to have a purpose and can lead to him being pushed away, which can lead to infidelity. Now by no way do I condone any unfaithfulness, but this is, unfortunately, the reality of this world.

If women of today realized how their independence is killing their relationship and the roles men play, didn't get caught up the superficiality of outward beauty over their inner glow and heal from past hurts in their life, they can become worthier of marriage for a future mate in their lives. They will attract higher quality men, nurture more fruitful relationships, and be more fulfilled overall in their everyday life. Let me say that this, not a foolproof plan; it is just some insights and steps a woman can go through to make that jump from side chick to **"Marriage Mate**

Contributing Author
Ernest "Cisco" Turpin

Ernest L. Turpin Jr is affectionately called Cisco. Cisco is originally from Charles City Va. and have since lived in San Diego and Memphis. He currently calls Jacksonville, FL home. Cisco is a Navy veteran and now works for the Federal Government, with a career in Aviation Communication and Information Technology.

Cisco is a lover, not a fighter with that he has two younger sisters and three daughters; he has spent his entire life around women that he loves, respects, and admires. Over his life span, he has closely learned about the perspective and views of the ladies. Cisco is an eligible bachelor. He was married twice; One union lasted for 16 years, the other for 14 years. With the adversity of divorce,

Cisco took a journey to identify the type of life, love, and relationships he wanted to experience. He comes to this book, not as an expert but a free- thinking man that looked in the mirror who did the work to become a whole, well-balanced man.

Cisco loves to read and to share ideas coupled with him being an advent golfer. Cisco initially began sharing his thoughts on social media (FB, IG) because he desired feedback and to give perspective. His shares gained him a captive audience eager for his insight and wisdom. His ideas, coupled with experiences, can and will help people. His honesty is welcomed and refreshing!

Please enjoy it as Cisco takes you on a journey in his eloquent writing!

CHAPTER 5

She Did Not Need A Man; She Wanted A Man

with
Cisco Turpin

The idea of choosing a wife is probably is the most crucial choice a man will make in his life. It will impact how successful he is as a father, career advancement, financial stability, and even his health. The selection of a life partner is one that can bring great joy or utter misery. With that being said, I am going to focus on the man and his thought process. The prerequisite knowledge and understanding of himself are required to make a wise and mutually beneficial marital union. I will share my perspective of needs and wants and how they both play their part in relationships.

Man

It is always a good practice to define terms when talking about any topic. Need is defined as something essential or significant. A need is vital to your survival, required for you to live your life or critical—the ability to understand what I need as a man and for that to matter. As a human, need is something that changes over time, not static, as I once believed. I have matured and evolved and now have a lot fewer needs because of growth and self-confidence.

Most men were raised to be the man, the breadwinner, the one the family depended on to provide and protect them. That is all well and fine, but if it is taken for granted, abused, or taken too far, it can be very damaging. I consider myself to be a man that needed to be needed, which was not a good thing. When you derive your self-esteem from role performance and feedback from others, you never truly live as a free person. You can do all the right things for the wrong reason; they look a lot alike but are different. Here is an example; a man can be faithful because he loves his wife, fear of punishment from God, or co-dependent. Knowing what we need in our life is good, and I think knowing why we need it is just as important.

The answer to the "why" of the need requires man to look at himself and dig deep to determine why he has that need. What is that need rooted in? What is driving that need? Examining if the demand was indeed a need or if it was a want and not a need at all? That man only answers those questions. Some of the answers make you feel good, and some will reveal pathology in thought. When those answers are brought to the surface is when the work begins. There, a man must be honest with himself and deal with the truth revealed that had driven his life; the good and bad. That old saying, "That is just way I am," has always bothered me. In my opinion, it means "I may be wrong, but

I am not going to do the work to change, so deal with it." When a man comes to terms with what he needs, his life changes, and he becomes very clear about who and why he is. It is no great sin to not know at times in his life but is a sin not to do the work to find out what he truly needs.

Now to move on to wants. Wants are things we desire, crave, or wish for in our lives by people or things. We should not only know what we want but why we want it. There is nothing wrong, enjoying a beautiful and attractive spouse if you desire them because of your attraction and appreciation. However, if your desire for a stunning spouse is to gain social status and the admiration of your friends or society, it is shallow and immature. You don't want the person because you love them; they are simply band-aids for your insecurity and lack of confidence. An even more harmful occurrence is when what you want is satisfied by something else randomly. That is when the people or things acquired to satisfy your wants loses its value. We soon become easily irritated and inconvenienced by the presence of those people and things in our lives.

What I have laid out is that a man must confront his needs and wants in his life. They have to be examined, and man has to be honest with himself and importance both in his life. Once a man can speak and walk in truth and communicate, he can fully navigate and identify any potential wife, saving both parties time, emotion, and energy.

Woman

Let me be obvious; these are my observations and thoughts; I do not claim to know how and why women think the way they do. Through conversation and asking questions, I will share what I have learned. Women are known to mature much younger and have a clearer picture of what they want and need. They seem to have a level of vision that is years ahead of men. In conversations with women, they will ask questions about your life plans, what you are looking for, and what your goals are. I imagine that is because most women have had those conversations with their parents or have talked amongst themselves. Regardless, they are years ahead of most men. That being said, I will speak on women's needs and wants.

I think two of the primary needs of a woman are security and protection. Those needs manifest in their desire for marriage or a stable relationship. Safety is usually desired in several areas: financial, emotional, and physical. Hence the search and competition for the handsome, rich, kind, sensitive man with a deep voice (bonus) who's faithful and loves only them if they can find all these traits in one man, generous! That would be perfect (joke)! A man to raise a family with, establish a home and build a legacy for the grandkids to talk about. Due to these needs, women often look for men with most of the traits to satisfy these needs. The ideal man is the man with the most boxes checked. I think women are so focused on the man to accomplish these goals that they will take on projects or men they feel have the potential to become the men they need in their lives.

They will work with that promise to do better or get it together. Those men tap into their nurturing nature and tell them, "I just need some to hold me down for a minute." Ironically. I don't see men as a whole offering the same assistance or patience.

I have also noticed once some women get the security, stability, and attention from the safe, stable man, they become bored. That is when their desire for excitement and adventure becomes very important to them; everyday life seems so confining and limited. The social media life comparisons to their friends or family living their posted (best experience) make them feel like life is passing them by. That relationship with the guy they could work with and build a life together now yields a life that seems empty and dull. Life's disappointing and hurts all play a part in these feelings.

Just like men, women must put those needs and wants on the table and examine them. They must dig

through the "why" about all of them. First, they must come to know their needs and how they want to get them met.

When that is settled, they can reflect on their wants and how to feel about them and what they are willing to give to satisfy them. That process is not quick and easy; it will bring tears and some lonely days. However, the clarity and power on the other side are exceptional and so peaceful.

Marriage

When a man and woman who are clear about their wants and needs sit down and communicate with each other honestly and sincerely, listening and caring about each other, they can rationally and calmly share how being together would make their life better. I say this because people should not add anyone to their life if it is not going to enhance their experience. Just because you love each does not make your lives a fit, and trying to force it with that "us against the world" mentality only works for so long. Eventually, the differences lead to anger and resentment. You will never know if someone loves you if they need you only. You see, needing a man and wanting to share your life with a man are two entirely different things. Needing a man is utilitarian, and enjoying a man is relational. A woman may need a man to pay her bills, fix her car, do the lawn work, help raise the kids or a host of other activities. That truth does not mean she wants his presence in her life as a partner or wants to know what he thinks. A man may need a woman to cook, clean, help with the bills, or look pretty at parties at his side, but that does not mean he wants an emotional connection relationship with her.

So, is it my contention that man and woman should seek partners that want to share and grow together with each one loving and learning from the other? Let trust, honesty, and respect be the foundation upon which attraction, intimacy, and loyalty can rest peacefully. We all want to be wanted and not a tolerated resource. Nothing is better than being liked, and nothing feels worse than being endured. So, choose the person that wants you in their life and not the one who needs you. Those are thoughts of a beige, country boy from Charles City, Va. The son of Joyce and Bootsy Turpin.

Extra

When a man hears a woman talk about her needs, sometimes he hears obligation, responsibility, and liability. Which to him, it seems like a job and the use of his resources to take care of a grown person whose lifestyle I am going to have to maintain or even upgrade just because we get married. Marriage is a business and legal contract that most people overlook or minimize because she wouldn't do me like that, or that is the type of man he is. You need to know the divorce laws in the state you live-"No-Fault" or "At Fault" divorce sates. Your lack of understanding can disadvantage you and leave you financially liable for many things you never imagined. So, in conversation, if a man hears about all the dreams the woman has post-marriage: trips, houses, cars, and clothes they will have, that is an excellent place to pause and think. Whatever lifestyle you accustom someone to, you may have to provide that ongoing. All I am saying is going into marriage, there should be no stone unturned, and a prenuptial agreement should be considered if there is an inequality of assets. If that offends anyone, then maybe you should find out why. If they came only to get their needs met, you best believe they are going after the resources to get them completed on the way out of the relationship.

Contributing Author
Darrin Baker

Darrin Baker is a Texas native originally hailing from Bryan, Texas. Darrin is a techie by day, but his passion lies with Modeling, Coaching at-risk youth, and mentoring. Darrin is also a part of a stellar nonprofit organization that provides scholarships for students who aspire to enter college.

Darrin is a vital leader of a political team designed to bring community awareness, positive change, and resources to the Houston and surrounding areas. He is also a talk show co-host and an avid golfer! This is Darrin's first-time creating magic in the pages of the book, and he looks forward too many more opportunities to let his marvelous light shine!

CHAPTER 6

He Wasn't Ready

With
Darrin Baker

Have you ever wondered why your man never chose you? Why wasn't he ready to settle down? Why, no matter what you did, it never seemed good enough? I know that you have gone back and forth in your mind as to what you were doing wrong. You may have even decided that he had someone else on the side, and that was why your relationship was at a standstill. The one thing that you may not have considered was in your face all along. Maybe, he wasn't ready.

The Mindset

From the time we are young and growing up, we look at our parents, and we watch how our mother treats us as kids. We remember how she cares for us, cooks for us, and feeds us, how she fusses at us, whoops us and praises us. All those things are what we look for in women. If it is useful when we find the result will be great for the future wife. And if the experience is not so great, we will have to create what we would like to have in a future wife.

Women always think that they know what is best for us. Some of them are right. Well, hell, most of them are. But we as men need to validate what is best for us. Sometimes we make the right decision, but most of the time, we make bad choices when it comes to women. That is why we revert to what we've known as kids. When it comes to men, women are mostly right, but we determine when we are willing to accept what they have to offer. We must be ready.

If you talk to us enough, we will tell you everything you need to know. We will tell you who we are as a person; our values, what we will and won't do for you or to you. If we don't talk a lot, our actions speak louder than our words ever could. Look at our habits: how we dress, how we treat you in public, and in private. Do we open doors for you? Are we polite? Can we hold a conversation with you and others? Can you keep us intrigued? How's your conversation? Are you respectful to my family? Again, we will let you know when the time is right. You can't tell us those things. We must be ready to accept what you see in us.

We, as men, are real simple animals. Some of us can take all day and never give anything back to you. Those are signs you should look for when choosing us. You cannot come into the relationship, knowing it all. You must create a space for us (men) to exist. We must feel needed from time to time. We need to be praised for the things we do for you. We don't want a "yes" woman all the time.

We want to know that you can be equal in the judgment of us and let us know when we are doing the wrong thing.

Every man looks for these qualities in a woman at different times in our life. A young man might look for someone he can have fun with. A girl that likes to have fun and go out every day. Very few young men look at the bigger picture when it comes to wifey material. You may not think much about these things, but you may want someone that feels a little like you. Someone who has the same thought process.

If you are a simple man, then you may want to find someone like-minded. If you happen to be a deep thinker, then you want someone that thinks that way also. Do they think of owning their own business? Can you do it together? Will she trust you to make business decisions? Will she support you in the new endeavor? Will she have your back when time gets tested? Is she a strong person who can handle herself in times of trouble? We, men, are firm most of the time, but sometimes we need to know we have a strong woman on our team if things get out of hand.

The only way to know this for sure is through communication. When he is ready to listen to what a woman has to offer, it is a sure sign that he is moving towards being prepared to creating something permanent in his life. If he is not a fan of communication, giving, or receiving, it's a sign that he is not ready.

When you have come of age, then you know what kind of women you want or even would like to have in your life permanently. When I was young, I didn't know what type of woman I wanted in my life. I was not even thinking about marriage. I just wanted to have fun, and I wanted to be with someone that wanted to have fun with me. As we mature and get older, we see many things; like how others treat women and how we as men should treat the women we want in our lives.

As we grow up, we see things differently. We want the necessary items. We want a freak in bed; we hope that she can cook and bring that paper home. For me, I took the path less traveled. I was married for a while, that relationship dissolved, and now I am looking all over again. I have seen them all: freaks, homebodies, businesswomen, strong and weak women. Some women think they have it all together. Some need a man in their lives, and some require the "good good" from men.

As I stated earlier, we are the one who decides when we are ready and who to choose to be our wife. The one bad thing about not being prepared is that some of us men miss out on a good thing. At that time, some of us are trying to have a good time and meet many different women. In doing so, we miss out on some great women. We are taught that we should have fun while we are young and get married after we have experienced life. When actually, we should probably marry young and save ourselves a lot of money and pain.

Men are straightforward creatures. We always look for the prettiest face and the body of a goddess. When all we need is someone that will love us, care for us, and have our backs when times get hard. All those physical attributes will fade away, and then we have what we needed, someone we can talk to and who listens to us. Someone to take long walks together with, to hold hands with, and reminisce about all the times that we have shared. We may talk about our children, where we will take our next vacation, or even gifts for our grandchildren. We will have the person who brings the stability, love, and quality to our lives that we always wanted but were afraid to pursue.

The Financials

In the process of looking for a wife, we want to be financially ready to be able to support the one we love. Sadly, some of us are not ready when it comes to this portion of the relationship. We have either gotten ourselves into some adverse financial situations, or we have never made any adult, lasting financial decisions, which is genuinely just as bad. Some guys leap before they look, others look before they leap. Either way, we wish to be able to provide for her and for any children that may come in the future. Guys want to get things accomplished and have a certain amount of dollars in the bank account. Some guys like to obtain those things alone, and others are looking for women to acquire those things together.

We want to look a certain way and drive a certain kind of car to attract a particular type of woman. As I stated before, we are the most smart-dumb people we know.

Sometimes that works out for us. Again, we must make that decision on who we choose and where we find them. Some guys want to have a house already and have things planned by the time they select the right one, or who they believe to be the right one. Then others don't have anything to offer, and we are hoping that once they get a wife, they can get all those things together and build it as one. We men look at our friends and their wives as examples. We see how their lives turn out, and either we follow the standard of how they acquire things, or we decide that the plan they chose is not going to work for us.

I will leave you with a few things. We spend a lot of time getting it wrong, but when we get it right, we are the luckiest men. The thing is this, once we've found the woman of our dreams, we've gotten lucky and chose the right one. But we have to be ready, and no woman can tell us when we are ready. As I look at it, sometimes we are not prepared for a relationship or entirely not prepared to give all we have to one woman.

We need a few things to work in our favor to make this love match work.

1. **Timing.** We have to be at a place in our life where we feel this woman can give us what we need when we need it.

2. **Age.** It plays a big part. As we get older, the better decisions we make with women. We see through a

lot of things. Contrary to belief, some women play games also. This is something that is sometimes missed when we are younger. Some women have a reason as to why they want us, and we don't have a desire to be with them. Instead of not being ready, this is being cautious. No man wants to become just a resource to a woman.

3. **Luck.** Sometimes there is true love out there. It may take a few times to get it right, but if you don't have success, you should try again if you'd like. "If you can't love the one you want, love the one you're with." Along the way, you might find the love of your life. I know that doesn't sound good, but that person may have something that you need in your life.

4. **God.** Pray on it, and it will happen. He will send that person to you in the most unlikely places, and you will never see it coming. LOL.

In the end, there is no way to know. Beauty fades away. So, keep living life, and maybe you will see something in someone, and you will have a beautiful marriage. Remember that a beautiful marriage is relative, and it is what you make of it. Being ready is a personal choice. No one can decide for us.

No one can "make us ready." As much as we would like to say by a specific time, a man should know what it is that he wants to do with his life, it's not necessarily a fact.

It takes some men longer than others, and some never mature to a degree of permanency in a relationship. But it is HIS choice, just as much as it is yours. If you feel that a man is not ready, it is up to you to decide what you want to do with YOUR time. If you think that a man is worth it, you may choose to wait. If not, you may walk away. But let it be your decision. Don't allow your emotions or attachment to someone to be a driving force to stay and

maybe miss out on the person that was truly meant for you.

Many men are ready, even if your current man is not.

Contributing Author
Nyatu Marvel

Nyatu is a true renaissance man, a well-traveled destination and restaurant connoisseur, with a penchant for tuxedos, supercharged German automobiles, and perfectly crafted martinis, he is known in many circles as the Black James Bond. He is a successful marketing consultant, investor, business owner, and developer with his hands in real estate investments, finance, the stock market, and the cigar and recreational cannabis industries. As a Relationship Consultant, Media Personality, and Public Speaker, his mantra is "Live Life on Purpose."

Formerly a Talent Manager in the Music and Entertainment Industry, Nyatu represented Multi-Platinum R&B Artist, Donnell Jones, iHeart Radio Personality, DJ Moondawg, artist and songwriter MARVO, co-writer of the hit *Sex Room* for Ludacris and Trey Songz, reaching

#69 on the US *Billboard* Hot 100, the then child actor, Michael Perkins, co-star of the movie *Hardball* alongside Keanu Reeves and music producers who created songs with Jay Z, Destiny's Child, Diddy, TLC, Missy Elliott, and Monica to name a few.

Nyatu is the former co-host of iHeart Radio Talk Show *He Said, She Said.* He sat on the *He Says/She Says* relationship panel at the 25th Anniversary of the Black Woman's Expo, Co-Moderated the Black Culture Week *Do You Still Believe in Black Love?* Community Discussion, the *Kiss & Tell* Relationship Panel Series, and numerous other relationship panels, talk radio shows, and podcasts.

He creates and champions content for his #DearFutureWife and #TheBlackMenAndWomenUnificationProject social media campaigns, to provide and promote positive energy, perspectives, and images of Black Love, Relationships, and Marriage, and to show Black Men the tremendous Value in Partnering with the right Black Woman.

CHAPTER 7

Sexual Compatibility

With
Nyatu Marvel

Being entangled with a woman we have excellent sexual compatibility and chemistry with is an incredible experience for a man. It's like finding our dream car and test driving it up the Pacific Coast Highway, on a beautiful sunny day, alongside the ocean in California, with our favorite tunes blasting through the speakers. At the same time, a hot woman goes down on us. It's like winning the sex lottery. It's exhilarating, it's an adrenaline rush, it's a shot in the arm, it's an ego boost, it raises morale, it makes Men feel more desirable, and most of all, it makes men feel like a "badass," and a "really great fuck." Every man wants to feel like a "badass" and a "really great fuck."

In the context of this book, "Why He Married Her & Played Me," let's explore sexual compatibility and how it may or may not play an essential role in men's choices in a wife. I think back to one of my all-time favorite comedies, "Harlem Nights" and the scene where after getting into an entanglement with Lela Rochon's character, "Sunshine," Richie calls home and says, "Hello, it's Daddy. Hey, darling, put Mommy on the phone. Yeah, Barbara, it's Richie. Yeah, look it, I ain't never coming home no more. Take it easy." In an earlier scene, Della Reese's character "Vera" proudly proclaims, "I've got a girl who's pussy is so good, if you threw it up in the air it would turn into sunshine" as all the Men in the room gaze into the air to imagine catching a glimpse of it. As the scenes comically suggest, a man that doesn't have excellent sexual compatibility with his woman will fantasize about, and may even cheat on her with or leave her for a woman with whom he does.

Now I am in no way, shape, or fashion, suggesting that excellent sexual compatibility and chemistry will keep a cheater from cheating or make a man that wants out stay. What I am saying is if you're going to be having sex, why not maximize and get the most out of your experiences?

What makes a man, or anyone for that matter, have an extraordinary sexual experience? I've learned that the ingredients or the litmus test for an unforgettable sexual experience include feeling great, before, during, and after sexual intercourse. The tri-factor. In addition to the physical pleasure, psychological and sometimes emotional pleasure must play a part in meeting the criteria for great sexual experiences, compatibility, and chemistry.

Sex is powerful... powerful enough to create life. There is so much that can come from exchanging and combining energies through sex. As with anything in life, there are levels to the sexual experience, different widths, and depths, it can get much more in-depth, and it can become

much more extensive and comprehensive. Sex can make you feel full of life and empowered like you can conquer the world, or it can make you feel dirty, inadequate, or stupid, and everything in between. Sex with the right person will have you feeling yourself. Sex with the wrong person will have you in your feelings. The anticipation of sex can have a woman "in heat" and dripping wet, it can make a man hard as a rock, or it can give either gender anxiety and fill them with dread. You can feel cosmic, energized, ready to go all night, or uninterested and just ready for it to be over.

Ask yourself these crucial questions. Why am I having sex? What are my sexual goals and desired outcomes? Am I focused on what I want to get or what I want to give? Am I enhancing the vibe, or am I killing it? Am I just giving my body, or am I sharing all of me? Am I tense in the bedroom, or am I the intensity in the bedroom? Am I striving to maximize our sexual experience, or just settling for the minimum?

Am I doing the same old routine, or do I put on a hell of a performance at my shows? What is my sexual mindset? What have the before, during, and after's been like for my man and me?

A woman once shared a story with me of a state trooper, pulling her over for speeding to meet her girlfriends for drinks. She immediately jumps out of the car to show her little black dress, heels, body, beat face, and hair... "Yes, Officer, I did whatever you say I did. I been bad all year long. Are you going make me put my hands on the car and spread my legs? (Places both hands on the car and spreads her legs) Are you going to search me for weapons? Are you going to arrest me, and put the cuffs on me, cause I'm into that." The Officer said, "Ma'am, please take your hands off the vehicle and get me your license and insurance." She said, "Aren't you going to take me to the station? Aren't you going to interrogate me and make me tell you all my dirty secrets? I need you to teach me a lesson. I need to be punished. Aren't you going to put your name and badge number on my arrest report?" The Officer said, "I'm serious now. Give me one reason I should let you off with just a warning." She said, "I don't want you to let me go. I want you to take me in the back of your car. I want you to take me to the station with you, so you can teach me a lesson, so you can punish me." Officer says, "Ma'am, you can go, get back in your car and slow down." She said, "Are you sure you don't want me in the back of your car?" with a wink. The Officer flushed red and chuckles, "Yes, I'm sure."

That was psychological warfare. Without even touching him, she literally and figuratively fucked his mind. I guarantee that Officer has fantasized a thousand times about what would have happened had he risked it all and took her up on her advances. Trust and believe; he has told that story to countless fellow officers, and every Officer responds the same way, "Get the fuck out of here? Really? Damn, I wish that had been me." I would bet the house that if he was married or had a girlfriend, he went home and role- played what his performance would have been if he did take her in the back of his squad car. You better know she asked him, "What got into you tonight?" Years later, I see similar stories floating around social media.

Now let me tell you a few things I know about that Officer, without me even knowing him. He felt attractive, desired, sexy, hot, risqué, flattered, excited, tickled, surprised, seduced, "eye-fucked," "mind fucked," sexualized, special, cool, etc. I dare say it made him a better police officer that night, certainly more cheerful. Twenty years from now, whenever he thinks about it, he will smile, he will blush, and he will chuckle while shaking his head. Five minutes of flirting and talking naughty created a memory that will last a lifetime. I shared that story to illustrate the energy and the anticipation that great psychological, sexual stimulation can make long before and after sex. Excellent sexual compatibility and chemistry don't have to be luck; it can be planted, it can be a well-placed spark, and it can be intentional. Sexual compatibility and chemistry are energy, and that energy is contagious. Excellent sexual compatibility and chemistry cannot be forced, but it can undoubtedly be coerced if you are aware and in control of your sexual energy.

Something as simple as a photo with a low-cut top asking about the color of your lipstick or a picture in your bra and panties asking how your new heels look. Music cannot be denied; make a super sexy playlist of the songs that give you the feels on Tidal. Send him raunchy songs with the hashtag #Mood. Men are suckers for a well-timed compliment or wink. Sexualize the way you eat your food in front of him. Use Google to find some cool sexually charged GIPHY's and Memes. There are even pictures of fruit that exude sexual energy. Be intentional, be creative, and be innovative.

Men want great sexual chemistry, be a got damn sexual chemist. Set him on fire. Give him something to remember before you give him some. The 5 P's hold even with sex; proper preparation prevents poor performance. Put some gas in his sex drive. Take and send him pictures when you shop for underwear. You don't even have to put them on. Find ways to create momentum going into your "entanglement" sessions. Dopamine is a hormone linked with motivation and reward. It increases sexual arousal, and the body secretes it. So, get the dopamine flowing. (SIDE NOTE: I hesitated to make the above suggestions because everyone is different. Some men would see those recommendations and hate every last one of them. Which is why the next paragraph is all about finding out exactly what your man is into.)

"The art of seduction is knowing what your lover wants and giving it to them in a way that takes their breath away." Like apps and operating systems, you must get sexual updates to have the latest version of your mate. Communication, communication, and more communication. Get your lover to open up about what they're really into. It might take some coercing to get all of the Intel. Please don't ask him during the game. Make the interview as sexy and sexual as you can if you know what I mean. Get it all! And I repeat, definitely don't ask him during the game.

Once you're clear on what types of things floats his boat, you have to put some effort into becoming a stand out at it. After all, if you have no desire to give your mate the best sexual experience, why are you entangled? This is the information age; you can learn how to be better at anything on the internet. There is a video instructional and Facebook group for everything. Whatever it is, you have to do it as you love it, and you have to do it like you have no morals. (DISCLAIMER: DO NOT DO ANYTHING THAT WILL COMPROMISE YOUR MENTAL, EMOTIONAL OR PHYSICAL HEALTH OR HAPPINESS.)

Be very passionate, be very enthusiastic, be very intense, and be very vocal. Tell him what you're going to do to him or what you want him to do to you. Channel your temptress energy. Make lots of penetrating eye contact. Find an intoxicating perfume to wear. Play songs that are a vibe and give you both the feels. Dance up on him. Grope him. Change the color of the lighting. Buy a reasonably priced mirror that you can whip out from time to time, place in the right spot, and tell him you want to watch him fuck you or him to watch you give him head in it. It's just like making your own porn but with no video or evidence left behind. Buy a sexy lace mask. Tell him there is another side of you that he hasn't tapped into and that you want him to bring it out of you. Put some respect on his name when you scream, moan and say it. Switch it up and use his last name, and call him Mr._! Play with your sexual power. Acknowledge his sexual power. Buy him a crown for $25 on Amazon and crown him King every now and then before going down on him. Buy yourself a crown and crown yourself Queen every now and then too. Initiate. Be assertive. Be spontaneous. Be naughty. Have fun. Feel amazing. Be amazing. "Talk that talk, honey, walk that walk money."

My hands-down favorite modern-day black love story is "Love Jones." My fellow Chicagoan Larenz Tate's character "Darius Lovehall" secured the bag and began creating excellent sexual compatibility and chemistry with Nia Long's character "Nina" the moment he stepped on stage and spit that sexually charged spoken-word piece written by another fellow Chicagoan, 6x Grammy award-winning artist Malik Yusef. "Say, baby, can I be your slave? I've got to admit, girl, you're the shit girl, and I am digging you like a grave... Right now, I'm the blues in your left thigh, trying to become the funk in your right. Is that all right?" All the Women in that room were picking up the sexual energy he was putting down. Darius doubled down when he convinced

Nina to go to reggae night at the Wild Hare, where he knew the norm was to grind on each other all night. He didn't leave the sexual compatibility and chemistry up to chance; he spoke it into existence and then manifested it.

Sexual compatibility can't be found in a dictionary. Excellent sexual compatibility and chemistry are that indescribable it factor that most of us are convinced you either have it or you don't. And that is true. But what most don't realize is that in many, if not most cases, someone decided to have and be that it factors. Someone has agreed to pay close attention, decided to read the body language, and listen to the bodies of their lovers. Either one of you or the both of you has decided to bring that energy to the connection. Someone has to choose to create the rhythm. Someone has to set the pace. Someone has to be sexually aware. Someone has to be the seducer. That someone might have to be you. Embrace it. During the arousal phase, the body releases Serotonin, which supports feelings of well- being and happiness. So, get the Serotonin flowing.

After, however, many rounds of sex, in a perfect world, all parties have orgasmed. Oxytocin is the love or bonding hormone, promoting feelings of intimacy and closeness. The body releases it after orgasm. Let the Oxytocin flow. Please don't ruin it by allowing your mind to wander and your mouth to introduce mood killers. Relax, stay present, bask in the afterglow of the moment, and avoid the wet spot. Compliment your lover on whatever he did well. Anything that stands out or that you particularly enjoyed, tell him how much you enjoyed it. If the next day or any other time in the future, you have a flashback or thoughts about the sex you just had, tell him all about your little walk down memory lane.

If you and your man enjoy cuddling, congratulations, soak up the euphoria that comes from the closeness, deeper connection, and intimacy. Many men and even some women experience a refractory period due to the oversensitivity of their genitals. If he isn't into cuddling or is short on time, don't overthink it or take it personally, grope him a couple of times for good measure and allow him to disengage.

Sex is meant to be freeing. It should open you up, not make you contract or close up. It is a passageway for synchronicity. It can and should be a spiritual endeavor. It's a rare opening for two souls to dance. Sex is exploration. Great sex is telepathy. Great sex is a rhythm. Great sex is a whole Vibe. In the course of writing this chapter, I had to put myself in a sexual space. I listened to my favorite playlist. I puffed on the best recreational cannabis. I sipped on a couple of bottles of Stella Rosa Black. My Sexual Energy began to expand, ex's started to call and text out of the blue, People who haven't conversed with me in years had visions of me writing and releasing books, invites to new entanglements found their way to me, I got a FaceTime from my 22-year-old Niece's, wanting to talk about sex out of the blue (I'm traumatized, we're all supposed to be virgins in our conversations with each other. LOL), etc. That is the Power of Purposeful Sexual Energy. I hope you enjoyed reading this as much as I enjoyed writing it.

Contributing Author
Chris White

Chris is a fitness expert and Master Trainer with an extreme passion for helping others reach their goals. He is a certified personal fitness chef, gym owner, and serial entrepreneur. He and his wife are the parents of five exceptional children. Chris has knowledge that goes beyond the gym as his life has exposed him to many different situations related to relationships. With his straightforward approach, Chris is sure to capture your attention and give you the brotherly love needed to help you navigate your relationships. Chris is an award-winning bodybuilder and an author of a fantastic cookbook that teaches the art of proper food consumption! In his spare time, he is an incredible actor and does stage places all over the Texas region. Chris is truly an All-American and well-rounded Guy!

CHAPTER 8

Social Compatibility

With
Chris White

Before we dive headfirst into how important social compatibility is when it comes to relationships, we must first understand what the term means. How do we define it? Is there a straightforward meaning to the word, or does it exist only on equal terms of respect for one another? It is valuable that couples enjoy the time they spend together. In my experience, relationships tend to excel when couples have companionship and a common interest in activities. With that stated, it is important to understand that couples will not have every interest in common. It would help if you did not assume that there is only one person that fits your idea of what comparability is. I know you may have heard this before, but you have several "soul mates." To think there is only one person that will compliment your idea of a relationship is honestly a naive way of thinking.

When you break it down, it is easy to understand how this thought process can block you from future blessings. Everyone has that one friend battling between "settling" and getting what they feel they deserve. They tend to reject potential partners before they genuinely get to know them purely based on how they look, talk, act, or their financial status. Being socially compatible is more about interpersonal traits and beliefs than money, looks, and image. I am not saying that money and appearance are unnecessary, but I am saying being socially compatible is just as crucial to a long-term relationship. What if the person you rejected because they didn't make enough money happened to have the same beliefs and a personality that was a good fit for yours? How would you ever know?

You can always find a way to make money, but you will not always be able to find that special someone that seems to connect with you so deep that material things seem irrelevant. The perfect man or woman does not exist; there is not one person on this earth that will share all your interests and meet all of the requirements you claim to need. We need to humble ourselves, try to create friendships first, and use broader spectrums of support. Eventually, we can learn to fulfill certain aspects that we may not have ourselves.

In any relationship, there will be work to do, and I want to acknowledge upfront that when people are with someone, they are not compatible with, they will not be happy in the long run. People do not always choose partners for the right reasons. Several different factors can play into this, for example, childhood and the environment. When we are growing up and learning the world, there are psychological walls that we build that limit the growth we

have as adults in our relationships. We seem to gravitate towards individuals that treat us like our family did, so naturally adapting can be a reasonably straightforward process. This is an unconscious level of thinking. We are programmed to seek people who are not ideal for us.

To give you some perspective, I have a friend named Pam that is the perfect example of this. Pam is a tranquil person, and she always seemed to date men just like her father, loud and charismatic. Now, this may seem okay on the surface, but she found she would never speak up for herself, and she always let the men make all the decisions. After a while, the men would dominate the relationship without her voicing her opinions. This was a recipe for disaster because she was in a situation where she never got what she wanted. In the beginning, this was comfortable for Pam because the pattern was based on the position she adopted from her family and childhood.

However, the reality is that she always ended up building resentment and even anger towards the men she dated, although at first, these traits seemed alluring. In essence, Pam became connected to a person based on unhealthy characteristics not compatible with her. The same reasons she gravitated to these types of men are the very reasons she ended up repelled by those same men. Do things flip and change, or was Pam negligent with the fact that she was attracted to someone whom she was not compatible with? How could a man with good values suddenly seem like he is judgmental? How could a person who seemed stable eventually be unstable? Someone she found charismatic now portrays narcissistic vibes.

My goal in this chapter is to help you avoid choosing a man for the wrong reasons, and even better, ignite an inner fire within you that seeks compatible relationships instead of surface traits. Let's dig deeper and look for men who challenge you and help you evolve into the best woman you can be. Let's take chances with relationships that enable you to receive the type of care that you deserve.

Reaching these heights will often put you outside of your comfort zone, but in the end, it will be worth it.

Consider my friend Pam again. Now she is married and about to have her first child with her husband. The man she married and the men she dated are entirely different. Her husband made her uncomfortable in many ways. He was not as good looking as the other men she dated; he wasn't a sharp dresser or highly charismatic. What he brought to the table was capability, a steady income, and a career with a solid head on his shoulders. What he brought to the table was what she needed but never received love, care, and a genuine interest in her wellbeing as a woman. Her family and friends liked him, he could go and support all her networking events, and they just flat out loved being around each other. Pam's story may have a fairy tale ending, but the experiences leading up to that ending are probably more of what you can relate to right now in your journey.

I want to help you reach your fairy tale ending by giving you thoughtful guidelines to start practicing when searching for a person who is socially compatible with you. This chapter will dissect social compatibility in 3 parts: the family and friend experiences, personality, and religious beliefs. I am going to give you insight on why putting unnecessary restrictions when choosing a partner can hurt you in the long run. Even if you get hurt in the process, it's better to be free-minded, not following your instinct to become unreasonable or create more complicated requirements for a future compatibility partner.

THE FAMILY AND FRIENDS EXPERIENCE

I believe the value in searching for dating patterns from your past endeavors can eventually work for you. Think about the good, the bad, and the ugly...what dynamics may have hurt your interpersonal relationship that may have caused family and friends to feel a certain way? How did you act towards your partner when you were around family and friends? Were you critical, controlling, or jealous? It may seem like I am placing blame on you, but I assure you that identifying your defenses and inner voices are critical to your growth. Furthermore, understanding the places and unhealthy situations that created them will take your current or future relationships to the next level.

When we bring up the toxicity of being around family and loved ones, we must acknowledge that our people expect certain things from us. Whether fair or unfair, these expectations have to be discussed with your partner beforehand so that an understanding can be reached between both parties involved. Do you know how your partner feels about your family and friends? When you communicate with mutual friends, do you both worry about impressions and specific challenges with social interaction?

Do you assume since it's your family and friends that everything is going to be fine and everyone will be comfortable? Let's keep it simple; if you have never taken the time in your past to notice this aspect of the relationship, this is the moment to analyze how past or current past partners may feel and react when socializing with family and friends.

By taking time out and critically thinking, you will separate the true you from the unhealthy wall you have formed from past experiences. Family can be some of the most brutal people to bring your man around. They have heavy opinions, and over time, this can change how you treat your partner. They can become critical of your choices because you have to acknowledge some of the bad and unrealized decisions in your relationship. Friends compare and even set ideological boundaries, but because we love our friends, their opinions matter to us. Often, it's hard to know if your family and friends have your best interest at heart or if they can separate their personal feelings enough to give you sound advice. I say, put less weight on their words and evaluate the boundaries you have. Like I mentioned before, look at your patterns. Do you keep the door open and welcome their opinions? If, however you have a habit of being easily swayed, don't even open the door. Listen to your intuition.

Do you feel uplifted in your relationship? Mutually taken care of and nurtured? These are the signals that say you are headed in the right direction. I can imagine when you first read the title of this section, you were expecting me to talk about your partner and how they need to be compatible with your family and friends. The truth of the matter is how you present your man, and the boundaries you set for your family and friends can determine how comparable he is with them. Ultimately, be vigilant of the business between you and your partner.

Always remember that family and friends may not be as forgiving when problems occur.

PERSONALITY

Are some types of personalities able to mesh more than others? What if we could predict who we get along with beforehand? I believe it is possible, and often we can find ourselves in a much more comfortable situation because we understand one another. Although we may be able to predict who we get along with, we cannot predict whether that will lead to a successful relationship or not.

We cannot specifically base a personality type on whether or not the relationship will work, but we can get a good idea of how we will interact with someone when issues concur. When dealing with love and the things that come with it, we long for this understanding, especially on the receiving end. We want to be able to share laughter and be best friends as well as lovers. We desire someone to listen to us and celebrate our victories in life. We want to feel protected by one whose characteristics fit closely with ours. This is natural and can lead to a stimulating relationship, but it is also flawed. We can desire these things so much and forget that there is no magic ingredient to the recipe of compatibility and relationships. It is something we have to be willing to work for and create. It is not given. Instead, it is an attitude and a state-of-mind about how you negotiate as you navigate along with your partner.

I am going to redefine the word compatibility by talking about personality. Often, we overuse the word "chemistry." Let's not get the two confused. Chemistry has no conscious connotation to it. We say things like, "We don't have to try, it's just there." Or, "It feels automatic when I'm with them." The problem is alluring and takes away our duty to examine and approach one another on a conscious level. Chemistry does not open us up and make us embrace unwavering qualities a person may have. Chemistry will only shine a positive light making it difficult to see the hard work of actually exploring, knowing, and respecting a person for who they indeed are. Since love operates on so many different platforms, we should strive for compatibility over chemistry to get involved in the complex task of biology and behavior. I feel you will operate best when you consciously shape your relationships with a compatibility mind frame. This is why personality is essential. Though people are sometimes attracted to different ones, it will help with your relationship skills if you understand the type that best suits you.

The first thing you should do is take a personality assessment. There are two in particular that I find gratifying. The first is the DISC test. This test will immediately help you improve your interpersonal skills. It will help you understand what you need to be the most successful. Note I stated to you, not your partner; this process is more about you than your significant other. You

always the problem or the one to blame, but we

must always look to ourselves first to see what actions we can take to better our chances of having a successful relationship. Understanding why you communicate the way you do can shine a light on some past and current issues you may be experiencing. The "why" is the single most powerful piece of information from this assessment because once you comprehend that, it becomes a choice on how you choose to move going forward. Remember, as I previously mentioned, true compatibility takes work and willingness on both ends. Before you get into a new relationship or exit a current one, you need to ask yourself; *Why do these things bother me? What can I do to shift how certain behaviors make me feel? Is it truly the other person's fault? And Can I try to understand them more?*

In the next assessment, I suggest you complete Myers Briggs 16 personalities.

This is my favorite assessment because it goes so far in depth that you end up learning things about yourself that you didn't even know. The accuracy is mind-blowing, and it can even help you in other relationships outside of your search for compatibility with your ones.

Though personality is not the only thing that matters in a relationship, it is a heavy hitter and can take your personal life to the next level if the work is put in. You've heard people say, "Opposites attract" and "Birds of a feather" these mean two different things, yet they both are right, but why? The underlying component is compatibility and how personality traits can be the source of attraction. Reflecting on specific personality traits will offer information about partners who complement each other, whether they are cut from the same cloth or two different tables. Let's look at specific personality traits and information you may find after taking your assessment.

- Openness to experience (has broad interests, imaginative, insightful) vs. Close-minded

- Agreeable (sympathetic, kind, affectionate) vs.Disagreeable

- Nervous (tense, moody, anxious) vs. Calm and Relaxed

- Conscientious (organized, thorough, planner) vs.Disorganized

- Extroverted (talkative, energetic, assertive) vs.Introverted

In life, connections through these traits are fueled by similar characteristics. As time moves on, those same traits may be less satisfying because your world is different. There may be kids, finances, and elderly families that enter the picture. While life will never be perfect, understand that any time life takes an unexpected turn, those same similarities or differences can make or break you.

It is time to break the mold and research you for you. Don't be afraid to embrace the work. After all, your personality is what makes you interesting; it is how we distinguish ourselves. Knowing and understanding your character can get you further in so many facets, and though it may change, it will never fade away. This is what people will remember about you.

RELIGION

What is the foundation of your relationship? Where is your source of comfort when good times and tension arise? When you're dating, I believe that avoiding in-depth discussions about the value of religion can be a mistake. I'm not saying during the first date, start reciting scripture. I am merely saying religious compatibility should be a top concern for many relationship seekers. The reality of it is that most people are more concerned with liking the same television series, sex, or outdoor social activities than they are religious beliefs. I am a Christian man myself, and

whether you pray to God, Allah, Buddha, Jehovah, or the sun gods is entirely up to you. Understanding that despite what your beliefs are, being in a relationship with someone who does not share the same views can cause significant tension. Having faith in something so intensely can be very attractive, but having differences can cause couples to struggle and create a lack of progress. Several studies suggest couples of different faiths are more likely to divorce later on because they ultimately do not share the same values. Have you asked yourself what you believe in and how your partner may respond to that? Interfaith couples do not argue about holidays, and their kids are more likely to have well-rounded futures. There are always, however, exceptions to the rules. On the same note, just because you marry someone of the same faith does not necessarily mean that you will enjoy a long-lasting relationship.

Though I have redefined compatibility, having a foundation of faith and a higher power can arguably be the most critical aspect of your relationship. After the sex dries up, the personality traits shift, after all of the family and friend experiences run their course, what are you left with? The answer is you and God. Before you can build with someone else, you must make sure that your spiritual armor is intact. It is natural to want to be involved with someone like-minded, and there is nothing wrong with having that preference if you are in line with the Creator. How were you raised, and what is your partner's background? Specific ideas have been taught to both of you, and some of those ideologies can lead to attitudes that are not healthy for any relationship. Often because of this, it is much easier to be involved with a person who is on the same wave as you religiously.

Religiously matched couples can pull from the same source that wouldn't be valuable without the spiritual bone during conflict or stress. Imagine a relationship where instead of arguing, you stopped and prayed together. WOW! This type of love and compatibility can only be shared when your religious provider and protector is the same. As much as we like to only think of the good times when it comes to marriage, a man wants to know and feel that through the dark times, such as losing his job, he can lean on his woman of faith to support him. It is so important for couples to believe in sanctification because that means you both share a sense of purpose that goes well beyond self-interest, family, friends, and even your kids. Sharing beliefs will enable you and your partner to facilitate the toughest of situations better than most.

Consider this. I have a friend named AJ, born and raised as a Christian, but the woman he was involved with was a Muslim. The conversation of religion came into play much later in their courtship, but ultimately, they had to have it.

As their relationship intensified, they began discussing the possibility of marriage. Someone had to make a decision. One of them had to convert to the other religion.

Her culture believed in Muslim law that does not allow Muslim women to marry non-Muslim men. The non-Muslim man would have to convert and show proof of his conversion to Islam. What I did not mention was that this relationship had already had a rough journey because AJ's mom never fully accepted his Muslim girlfriend. She put extreme pressure on him to end the relationship. His girlfriend was putting undue pressure on him to convert to Islam.

What was he to do? Sure, they got along and were compatible in other ways, but not one of the most important ways. How could AJ convert to something he didn't believe in to be with her? Why would any woman want a man to convert from what he believes in to be with her? Wouldn't this build resentment down the line? You can see how there would be so many layers to this decision and why I want to help you avoid it. In the end, no one converted, and the relationship ended. They invested years in a situation that was doomed from the start. We cannot be afraid to seek comfort in knowing that we believe in the same things our partners do.

Religion gives order and peace during the chaos, so most relationships that lack these two qualities quickly fade. Sharing the same visions and values are true components to being successful in your relationships. Remember to establish yourself first in Christ or the God you believe in and then seek a partner who believes in that entity as you do. This is the eternal force that will keep people together for the long haul.

CONCLUSION

Beginning from the dating process and then following into marriage, issues of compatibility can take its toll on relationships.

We toss the word compatible around a lot in conversations with others about whether we should end or continue our relationship. I hope you have a better understanding of why these conversations should occur when considering your next move. Every relationship we ever engage in will need to have some feeling of trust and commonality mixed with nurturing emotions. We form these feelings throughout our lifetime, and often our true nature is seen differently in a social context.

Society won't always know what we've been through, and sometimes we do not know ourselves. The tools I have given you in this chapter should help you to identify some of your attributes that may have been holding you back from the best relationship you could ever encounter.

Do not make the mistake of thinking that you can change the other person just because you understand why they are the way they are. You cannot adjust when there is incompatibility; instead, focus on consciously recognizing the true attributes that would mesh well with you to make your journey easier.

Contributing Author
Joseph Carey

Joe is a native of Baltimore, Maryland, currently resides in Jacksonville, Florida. He is a graduate of Northeastern University in Boston, Massachusetts, where he received his bachelor's degree in Sociology. While at Northeastern, he was also a member of the Men's Basketball team. Joe is a 23-year veteran in the investment and insurance industry. He is the President of Slight Edge Financial Inc. and a consecutive Million Dollar Round Table producer (MDRT). He is most passionate about at-risk youth, humanitarian efforts, civil rights initiatives, fighting against poverty, financial literacy, and spiritual awakening.

CHAPTER 9

Spiritual Connection

with
oseph Carey

A spiritual connection has been described in many ways by many people. I will speak on what this means to me at this point in my journey called life. The spiritual connection between a man and a woman doesn't just mean believing in the same religion. We've seen, and I have experienced that professing the same belief in a "God" isn't the "glue" that makes a relationship or union last. It doesn't even make people like each other, but that's a whole different conversation! What do the two words mean?

Let's examine:

Spiritual: relating to or affecting the human spirit or soul as opposed to material or physical things.

Connection: a relationship in which a person, thing, or idea is linked or associated with something else.

A relation of personal intimacy.

An arrangement to execute orders or advance the interests of another.

When you look at those definitions, a lot comes to mind. Yet, the third definition of CONNECTION sticks out like a "sore thumb." I believe that meaning is what is lacking most when it comes to the spiritual connection that I've experienced and possibly many others. So many go into relationships more focused upon what the other person is going to provide for them.

The false expectations of being taken care of, not about their responsibility of promoting the other person's interests and allowing space for the same to be reciprocated.

I was in a twelve-year marriage that had the look of a great spiritual connection, but it was nothing but a shell! It was a relationship that went through the motions and a marriage done for the wrong reasons. We had religious compatibility, but that was all it was. She wanted me to be what she thought she needed to complete her and coax her insecurities, which were many. I wanted to be her hero and save her. To love away her insecurities and hoping she would feel better about herself, straight bullsh*^t! It wasn't either of our responsibilities to provide any of that to each other. Those expectations were false and exhausting. The softness and cohesion that we wanted were non-existent and, ultimately, what caused the demise of the marriage. I tried to save someone that I couldn't save. She wanted someone to do her heavy lifting of genuinely loving herself and make her happy. That was insanity! The gift we denied ourselves was a real spiritual connection, and I guess I had to go through not having that connection to learn what it truly is. Now I know, and I am still learning the truth of what true spiritual connection is. I'm learning to work at it with myself and making myself open to receive it.

So, let's talk about what spiritual connection is. I would say to first get religion out of the way. It hinders things and legalizes too much to think unconditionally. Spiritual connection, logically, it cannot be seen, yet it can only be felt. It is a divine or universal force that attracts you to another human being. You may not have ever met this person. You instantly recognize that you have something in common. You don't know what it is, but you feel like that person is a part of your being. This person is a part of your being on a spiritual level, not religious but spiritual.

Every single one of us is made of energy, and this energy is turned into vibrations. Some people have lower vibrations, while others have very high vibrations. I have a high vibration, didn't always have it, and I work every day to keep it vibrating high. These vibrations are affected by lifestyle, beliefs, perceptions, values, etc. the Creator has given us gifts, talents, and abilities. The Creator will not do the work for you. The Creator will not help or save you from yourself. Our responsibility is to remember from which we come and stand in the power that we have been endowed with. Things that happened to us may or may not be our fault, but our responsibility is to get past it to be better and do better. This is where we begin to establish a spiritual connection with ourselves and develop into who we are. Sadly, many of us don't do this work of vulnerability and carry these issues into relationships and depending on the person in the relationship to bear the burden of your unfinished inner work.

Ultimately, we lose the relationship because there was never a genuine connection. After all, one or both of you never spiritually connected with yourself. From here, we're going to touch on characteristics of spiritual connection, what does it look like, what does it feel like, and what happens that confirms that it is a spiritual connection.

A spiritual connection is evident when a couple experiences harmony, understanding, and peace. Emotions come deep from within the core of the heart, physically and mentally. Relationships born out of spiritual connection "compliment" our needs as it aids us to develop into a higher version of ourselves. The big key in spiritual connections is what you desire in the other person!

Let's touch on some areas that play crucial roles in developing and knowing that you have a spiritual connection.

1. You're Comfortable in His Presence

Being spiritually connected to someone creates a certain peacefulness when you're around this person: no anxiety, no pressure, no façades. You feel safe to be your true self, no masks. You don't feel uneasy at all. It's like you just let down your total guard.

2. Your Authentic with Him, Knowing Vulnerability Is A Strength

You let him see you naked, stripped of your makeup, stripped of your clothing, stripped of all the fraudulent things and attitudes you wear around strangers. Wigs weave etc. You get the picture. He knows every inch of you. Communicate with curiosity, common ground, and connection as the primary goal. Don't use this as the "spy time" to indulge insecurities you have or are working on; it will be a "slow kill" to the relationship. Practice being able to converse, have conflict, and come together again with a strong sense that you belong together even through disagreements. Work on remaining open and vulnerable as this would deepen overstanding and respect in the relationship. Most of all, don't drive a wedge between you two by holding grudges and stoking resentment. Passion and friendship will be both boosted by a willingness to come together to repair your relationship when necessary.

If you and your partner emphatically listen to each other and "overstand" each other on a deeper level, it's another sign of deep spiritual connection. If you have that feeling that you can tell your partner anything that comes to your mind and you know he will not find himself offended or annoyed, it means you trust him, and he's spiritually connected, he also trusts you. Relationships without authenticity and trust are doomed to fail!

3. There's Mutual Respect Between the Two of You

Another sign of a deep spiritual connection is Mutual Respect. Mutual respect means respecting each other on many different levels. It means respecting each other's "flaws," freedom, differences, similarities, etc...... and always giving some space to your partner for his emotional growth. This should be reciprocal. If you and your partner don't have a problem with respecting each other's personal space and celebrating each other's differences and similarities instead of continually trying to change each other, you have a healthy relationship that is blessed with a deep spiritual connection. To be able to respect each other, you have to have open minds and open souls. Respect comes from within, and it is one of the most potent traits one can

have.

4. Your Conversations Are Unstoppable

You two converse on many topics, and you lose track of time. You start talking, and the next thing you know its hours later. It's as though there's only you two left in the world, everything and everyone around you disappears. I call it being present. You can talk and talk and talk about any topic. You two are intellectually attracted to each other. You don't always talk about it discuss surface topics. You converse about in-depth, stimulating topics such as spirituality, purpose, business goals, politics, and other issues that are bigger than the two of you. It enriches the relationship and works toward deepening the spiritual connection.

5. Laughter Is Always Around

Your sense of humor is similar; you two are swapping smiles. You can joke with each other; you can playfully joke and pick at one another.

You two can laugh at yourselves and others respectfully. You appreciate the humor in life, generally speaking. When you're together, the world feels lighter. Less morbid. More hopeful.

6. You Two Have Similar Minds & Morals

While you two won't think alike always, there are many similarities on those "make or break" focuses like social stances, political, spiritual, financial, to name a few. Again, while they may not always be 100% alike all the time, they are close and healthy compromises can be made.

When they are opposite, the ability to "agree to disagree" peacefully will be a sign of a deep spiritual connection. Being able to respect differences is crucial to a sustainable spiritual connection! You two have similarities in your moral convictions. Whether its civil rights, environmental issues, political stances, financial pursuits, etc. You two stand together and complement these morals that you see eye to eye on or pretty close. It would be almost like you both see through the same goggles. Talking to one is almost as if you are talking to both.

7. You're Feelings for Him Are Inexpressible

You can list things you love about him, but you can't articulate why your relationship works with absolute accuracy; it just does. There's something about your love and admiration for him that goes beyond the spoken word.

Your girlfriends, family members, or colleagues may not "overstand," but you two do, and that's all that matters!

8. Every Touch Comes Naturally

Your bodies have a natural rhythm. The simple touch is an energy you can't explain. Just a simple hug, kiss, love tap is magical. Cuddling, sex, caressing is exhilarating and beyond satisfying. The energy that this person has can be felt through and through when they are just near.

When they touch you, you get all tingly and little girl like. Even when you want to be mad at them, they can touch you, and you cave!! This is what touch in a deeply spiritual connected relationship can exhibit.

9. You Can Sense When Something Is Wrong

He never has to verbalize that he's had a bad day. When he walks through the door or calls you after work, a meeting, or whatever his vocation is, you can tell if things went his way or not. If you're connected, you can feel if he's in trouble, not feeling well, had a bad day, etc. Very few couples achieve this level of spiritual connection, hence the number of divorces and broken relationships.

If you're connected this way, I'm betting that all aspects of the relationship are firing on all cylinders regardless of the title!!

Everything Feels Easier When You're with Him, Even When You're Not

Sometimes you disagree, sometimes you argue. Sometimes, it's hard to hold on to your love, but most of the time, things are pretty straightforward. Everything flows. It's not fake or going through the motions; you two work well together. Whether it's handling life or doing pleasurable things, it's like second nature to you two. Things feel right, even if things seem to be going wrong. There's no other way to explain it!

10. He Helps You Heal

He's always by your side with bandages or salves, ready to help you seal up any wounds the universe inflicts. He isn't your savior; the reason your body and mind find the will to breathe, but he inspires you to save yourself. He reminds you who you are, your gifts, talents, and abilities.

He reminds you why your life is worth it and why you play an essential part in the world. He reminds you what you mean to yourself, your loved ones, and him.

He reminds you how strong you are and how you've even motivated him at times. He reminds you that the love you have to give and receive is worth going another mile.

11. Your Intimacy Consists of More Than Just Sex

Intimacy, contrary to popular belief, is far more than sex. Intimacy comes in many varieties. Learning your partner is intimacy; it lets him know that you're genuinely into them and want to "overstand" them fully. Doing things outside the bedroom together is intimacy and sets the stage for sexual connection.

These acts of intimacy outside of the sexual act creates bonding and educational opportunities for the two of you to learn more about your partner. It helps discover likes and dislikes; it promotes more profound vulnerabilities that can become strengthening tools for you as individuals and together. Here are some ways to grow and maintain intimacy in your relationship outside of sex.

A. Pillow talk, cuddling

Before life rushes in to steal you two away from each other, roll over for face-to-face communication. This looks different today with technology, so you may give a morning call or text if you aren't cohabitating. I've heard of couples praying together, reading devotionals, or just discussing what their day will bring and the two encouraging each other before the start of it. Sometimes it's the opposite; it's talking the day down, discussing what happened that day and providing encouragement or just being an ear for your partner, letting them positively vent.

B. Ensure That Fond Feelings Flourish

Root out the tendency to criticize and nitpick. Keep each other's positive characteristics and attributes in the forefront of your minds.

Express more positivity than negativity. Compliment and celebrate your partner. Accept each other's "flaws" with grace and love. Maintain the fact that you like each other! Build upon and continue to grow the love between you two in word and deed.

C. Use Your Tech to Touch Base

Technology is a crucial source of communication these days. Use it to your advantage and towards the growth of your relationship. Our screens tend to distract and divide our attention, steal intimate moments using your screens. Take charge of your tech and charge or recharge your intimacy in the relationship. Put it to work daily. Send love texts, use avatars to send love messages, check on him throughout the day, be creative. Hopefully, this is being reciprocated?!

D. Don't Hold Back the Gratitude

Show and tell him how much you appreciate him. It strengthens the bond! It also can help toward thinking more highly of each other and what is being created along with the value of it.

E. Do Activities Together

Doing fun cooperative activities such as; a new recipe, a DIY project, picnic, hike, exercising together, or whatever "floats your boat." These are things that inspire intimacy in a relationship and make the sexual experience deeper!

12. The Sex Is Fire!

Another sign of a deep spiritual connection is intimate sex. Intimate sex or making love is much more than just having intercourse. It's Soul Sex!! Being intimate with this person means giving yourself entirely to him without the fear of being judged or rejected. This feeling of deep intimacy is so powerful; you feel healed, drained, and replenished all at once. Every time is like the first time. Many different emotions are expressed like crying, screaming, and trying to catch your breath.

The feelings that go on during this moment are unexplainable! It could be one or all these. It's more than just enjoying your partner's body. It's connecting two souls into one. It's the truest form of vulnerability towards your partner. You are not afraid to admit that you're scared when you are, and you're not scared to show your partner how much you love and care for him. You want them in your life regardless of title.

Honorable Mention Author
Pastor Marques D. Neal

Marques D. Neal is the Founder and Senior Pastor of an innovative and progressive ministry located in Temple Hills, Maryland. Lion of Judah, known as "The Kingdom Church," was established in April 2004. Pastor Neal has over 25 years of sacrificial service. He is a visionary leader, anointed to teach and preach the Word of God with simplicity and vigor.

Pastor Neal is a highly sought-after preacher, speaker, seminar moderator, and author. He is recognized internationally for his unique ability to equip men, women, and youth for leadership in the work of the Lord. His passion is to see men restored, women uplifted, and mend destroyed, estranged, and broken families back together. His ministry has touched many lives. He has a heart for outreach, and you will often hear him say, "It's not what's in these four walls that matters.

We are here to get equipped, to go out and reach those that no one else will bother to reach, and love on them as Christ loved us."

Pastor Neal has appeared on multiple media outlets, including "The Greg Davis Show," "The Word Network," "The Impact Network," and "The Lady O Show." He attended the Bible seminary at Howard University, Bible catechism training at Bible Way Temple, Washington Bible Seminary, and the University of Phoenix. He is also the author of "How to Make the SHIPS Work" Friendships / Relationships - Tools for A Successful Journey.

Pastor Neal is married to Co-Pastor Lisa and is the proud father of five anointed vessels: Donovan, Michael, Princess, Marques II, and Sidney II and grandfather of one adorable granddaughter, Harmony. He is a firm believer that charity begins at home and is an avid advocate of family values.

The Conclusion Of The Matter

With
Marques D. Neal

#1 – SHE LEARNED ME TO EARN ME

Understand this; those that take the time will always get the treasure! Ladies still hold on to this…. anything worth having should never be rushed. You will ruin it if you don't get this! Take your time and learn everything you can about him. Gain the knowledge you will need to be in a relationship with him to help build with him. Study him, with him and for him. Study him – pay attention to what he says, how he acts, and how he moves. This will be important as you move forward. Study with him – He needs to know that the woman he has is always willing to develop as he develops. One of the worst feelings for a man is to feel like he's becoming, and his lady is two steps behind. Study for him – Know how to do your part. Your parts are the things that get his attention and lets him see there's something different about you. As you are learning him, you will understand the necessary adjustments that must be made.

Now, remember, you are doing this because, in the end, it's what you wanted. The woman that gets this is the woman that will earn him. You can't get the interest of a man if you can't get a man to be intrigued. Can you arouse him, get the curiosity of him, have him make secret plans to do something for you? Trust me, those that take the time will always get the treasure – the quality of a man, his passion and possession, his mental ability. He will ever think of you and for you. Thinking of you - what you mean to him and how valuable you are for him.

Thinking for you - he will always be thinking what could he do for you today to make your day an unforgettable one and your life a much deserving one. The one that learns is the one that always earns.

Here's a tip to take – the student that lives a good life is the one that comes to understand, pays attention, knows when to take and ask questions, can follow instructions, does their homework, and pass their test. Take the time, and you will get the treasure. She learned him, that's how she earned him!

#2 YOU NEVER GAVE HIM A REASON TO COMMIT

Ok, well, where do I begin with this here. Be careful about what you give because you may not get what you want. Don't be so fast! There's an old saying, speed kills, and that still stands true today. If you keep giving everything, you might end up getting nothing. A real man loves the chase. If you take the hunt from him to pursue, then you take the conquer from him - to overcome, to take control of, to gain the love, to respect.

Here's a tip to take - every lion goes after what he feels is worth it. When he feels it's what he wants, it's your worth his wants! What's the reason for him wanting or not liking you? Your actions, your mind, your understanding, your processes? How do you act for real? Where is your mind at? Do you understand, and what was your process of interpretation? How did you get here? Furthermore, why are you here?

For a man, the reason has to be reliability. Reliability – the quality, the trustworthiness, the consistency, the quality of what he's getting. Will this last? The dependability, will this work? The character, will she submit? Now please don't trip off the word submit; it only means accepting the authority!

Here's another tip to take – you can't get or keep a man if you are the man you want! He must be able to count on you for him to commit, be fully dedicated, and obligated. Every real man wants to commit, but you must give him a reason.

A man will commit where it has been made comfortable. In the Bible, the book of Judges, Chapter 16, Samson commits in the comfort of Delilah's lap. Although she took advantage of him, the point is, he found a place of surety - the state of being sure and confident.

When a man commits, he's saying I'm now comfortable, and when this happens, don't use it against him but use it to adore him, love him and respect him. Be careful of what you are giving because it might not get you what you want. In the race of the rabbit and the turtle, the rabbit was moving fast. He felt he could stop and rest. The turtle moving slow knew he had to stay responsible and keep going. In the end, when he woke up, he saw the turtle crossing the finish line.

Here's another tip to take - maybe she got him because she remained responsible to him, and perhaps you lost out because you felt what you were doing was good enough, and you decided to stop and take a rest. If you haven't given him a reason, why should he commit? If you keep switching up on him eventually, he is going to turn the switch off, and then it's a good night and goodbye!

#3 YOU ARE A PLACEHOLDER, NOT A PARTNER

You were good for that but not good enough for this! This can get tricky and very sensitive, so please don't kill the messenger. Now, here's the thing, it was the requirements that led to the rejection! Take a deep breath on this one. A placeholder has its place but doesn't have what it takes to be permanent, at least not yet. Let me give you my personal experience. I worked in the school system as a Substitute Teacher.

I got so good at what I did; they made me a Teacher's Aide. No matter how good I was or how much the staff, the Principal, or the students liked me, I was nothing but a place holder - something used temporarily to substitute for something else. I held the place for what was to come later because I didn't have the requirements - something wanted, needed, or necessary.

They knew that I was someone they could use when and where they wanted to put me or place me, whether I liked it or not. I still showed up every day because I needed them just like they needed me. Regardless if it was only for a moment or two until what they wanted either came in or came back. I didn't have specific requirements, so no matter what they felt for me, they could not make me a partner and certainly couldn't commit to me because I had not put myself on that level.

I was good, just not good enough. I didn't put myself in place to compete, so I was rejected, dismissed, refused, and overlooked. And it wasn't their fault; it was mine because I became content and complacent with being a placeholder. I never did what was necessary to become a necessity. I never got what was required to be wanted or needed; I was someone they knew they could use on their terms. The problem with the placeholder, let's call them the Teacher's Aide, it's a lot of them out there in the system waiting to be used. The partners, let's call them Teachers, are not enough, and they are so needed.

Here's a tip to take - if you don't have the requirements that he needs, you will get rejected not because he doesn't have feelings for you but because you don't have what it takes to fill the partner position.

#4 YOU WERE NOT MARRIAGE MATERIAL

We are in a time where everybody wants to be married, not understanding what makes a marriage.

What it is has nothing to do with you but has everything to do with the other person. Did you ever stop and think that maybe you weren't marriage material because what he was missing you were lacking?! What makes a building what it is? The material used to make it what it was not. Now read that twice! Ask yourself, do you have the material – the physical, the spiritual, the mental, the relevance to help take him from what he is not into what he will be and helping him make good on what exists in his life because you are essential for his life. You have to become that critical part that he cannot do without.

Here's is a tip to take - being married, you become the source - that which something comes from, for him to be able to see his seed. Man gives her his seed; she births him a baby. Man gives her his dreams; she births him his destiny. What can you put out after he pours into you? I think before considering becoming a bride, every woman should ask herself what your capabilities to giving birth to every area of his life are? What material are you bringing to the job called marriage? Adam sacrificed a rib that God makes into a woman that Adam calls help material that helps the blueprint become a reality. It takes it from what it is and turns it, the blueprint, into what it was not - reality a building. Maybe you were not marriage material because he felt like he couldn't build with you. That what he was missing, you were lacking, and there could be no future. Marriage is more than just a ring and a wedding day. It's about being right for each other and putting in the work every day.

#5 SHE DIDN'T NEED A MAN SHE WANTED ONE

This is a major! What this is saying is she did what she had to do, not expecting him to have to do it for her. In other words, he didn't have to come in being her savior, but he could come in being her soulmate!

One of the greatest feelings for a man is to know that she wants him out of a desire. Not that she needs him out of desperation! When there is a desire - an intense craving and yearning, to have a man, it all comes together and is perfect. Desperation is the despair that will result in a rash or extreme behavior. Once a man comes in as a savior, you will always need him as a savior. If he ever gets to the place where he can no longer operate as a savior, then her behavior will become too irrational - not being able to think, sensibly, or even logically because she needed him, but when she wants him, he can become her soulmate. Making sure she remains in a safe place, a connection of the minds, mutual respect, unconditional love, and understanding her being able to be herself and him understanding her thoughts and being right there with her walking side by side. He will listen to her with all his heart and all his head, and he will know just the right things to say and do.

He will know when a kind word is needed, or no comments are needed at all. He will learn how to fill the void to make her feel safe and loved.

Here's a tip to take - every man wants to feel like he fits perfectly into where you are and what you have. He doesn't want to fight for a place in where you are and what you have, where you want him and not need him. He doesn't have to be your superhero but your haven.

#6 HE WASN'T READY

Knowing when a man is not ready or not prepared will save you a life of pain. This has two problems. When a man is not prepared, a woman, at times, can try to force him into something he doesn't want, or she begins to think or feel like something is wrong with her. She asks questions like, why aren't you ready or what's wrong with me?

Ladies, nothing could be wrong with you, he is not prepared, and that is ok. Consider this - he might not want a relationship right now. Maybe he wants to focus on other aspects of his life that he might not be happy with, and he's having a hard time expressing that with you or anybody. He might not know how to communicate effectively, or he's not over his last relationship yet.

Giving a man the time, he needs could be the very thing that saves you from torture. Sometimes ladies can get to a place where they want what they want when they want it, so they start to give the man ultimatums, demands, and terms like if you don't, then I won't. Well, ultimately, that will cause the man to begin to breakdown and then shut down. If a man ever says to you, he is not ready to trust me to take his word, he is not, and nothing you can say or do will make him ready. It's him and within him. It's what he has to deal with.

He needs to know that he can count on you to stand with him and support him, not pressure him or penalize him for where he is or what he feels, thinks, and believes he needs to do to get himself to a place where he is ready to take that step.

Here's a tip to take - if you ever put a man in a place he doesn't want to be, he will cause you pain you could have never believed.

#7 SEXUAL COMPATIBILITY

I don't think males or females genuinely understand how serious and important it is to be sexually compatible. To not be sexually compatible is like walking with two left shoes on. Give it time that will get very uncomfortable, and once they become irritated, they will soon become unhappy. Not being able to satisfy him could be what's separating him. The bedroom could be the breaking point.

When you have compatibility, what you are saying is you have two things that can exist or occur together without problems or conflict. Please take the time to read that twice. Where there is no sexual compatibility, it will always become difficult for you to exist, and if you can't exist, the exit will follow.

The two being together will most definitely be a problem or conflict. Being able to keep up is essential to being able to keep things together. I don't care what anyone says being sexually compatible is major.

Let me share this, no man wakes up one day and says, oh, I think I'm going to cheat today! No, it doesn't happen that way. It happens because, over time, he has dealt with not being satisfied, and he has reached a point where he is fed up, so the search begins. Not having sexual compatibility in the bedroom could be a deal-breaker. There has to be a connection. You must be open, honest, and transparent when having conversations.

If there are different sexual expectations and wants, and it is not addressed, he could become resentful, which leads to him being sexless. Or should I say sexless with you. Be sure you know his turn on and his turn-offs emotionally, cognitively, and behaviorally.

Sexual compatibility can come down to what he believes, needs, and desires.

You have to be sure you will be able to mesh and be able to keep up.

Here's a tip to take - you can't bring a lion home and treat him like a dog! That's not going to work. News flash, it's a lion! Attend to it as such. No man wants to feel like he's getting what he needs to satisfy him to find out later he was deceived. That's like paying your money for something name brand only to find out it's a knockoff.

He wants to know that he is on the same page with the woman he is with when it comes to the structure of the relationship regarding the bedroom because if sexual compatibility is a problem, he might start pursing the answer elsewhere.

#8 SOCIAL COMPATIBILITY

This is simply the state of having the capability to communicate in any setting. If a man feels there isn't a certain level of communication, it's not going to be complete for him. How are the living conditions? What is he coming home to? What is the environment like for him? How do you fit in the characteristic experiences for him? The person you are, the places he goes, and the things he does. When a man feels like he is forcing you to fit in this frame for him, the picture he sees will always be distorted.

Here's a tip to take - if you can't see it, you will always struggle. In dealing with social compatibility, the experience must be explainable. It must be clear to him. It must make sense to him. It has to be a motivating factor for him, how he lives, and where he lives and the woman fitting into it. Behavior and interaction must be functional. If he is consistently frustrated, this could be the finish of any relationship. It is being able to operate equally on the same level in group functions. How does she carry herself? How does she present herself? Is she able to keep up? If this is off balance and he feels embarrassed, this will be a significant strain on the relationship and how he could feel moving forward. Let me help you. One of the most beautiful things for a man is to know his woman has the ability of a chameleon. She can be distinctive and highly specialized, having the ability to change colors, which means knowing how to fit in where they are. To say it like it is, a man wants a woman in the street but a freak in the bed.

Social wellness is the strength of having and building together respect, trust, and friendship. There must be social compatibility if it's going to be complete. Please don't kill his vibe! Be the person in his picture that makes it what he wants to see.

#9 SPIRITUAL CONNECTION

I can't begin to stress how vital, necessary, and important the understanding of having this is if you want the relationship to work and last. Having a spiritual connection is what's going to keep the relationship together. He has to know that he has a woman that is tapped in spiritually for him, and that can be that rock when things get rough.

Here's a tip to take - every man will get weak from time to time, but there's nothing like knowing you have a woman that can encourage you during those times. When there is a spiritual connection, you know just what to speak when dealing with any situation in life. Proverbs 18:21 says, "death and life are in the power of the tongue." In other words, what comes out of your mouth can either kill or give life. There's an understanding that the tongue serves as the treatment to their totality, the whole of something. When you can see where a person is spiritual, you can tell how they will treat you. Having a spiritual connection means that there's an experience of Harmony, understanding, and peace. Here is where the emotions come deep from within the core of the heart.

Whenever things are off spiritually, there will always be a problem physically, mentally, and emotionally. Amos 3:3 says, "can two walk together except they be agreed?" Question for you: How are you going to make it when you are walking with someone that is a spiritual mistake? Let's look at this closely. Here walk means - to move at a regular pace. Spiritual connection says that we are always moving, always pushing forward.

Why? Because we should be walking by faith, not by what we see in the physical form. Next, is the word together – combination, as one. When there is a spiritual connection, there is no division. It's one accord, thinking the same thing and speaking the same thing, operating in complete unity. Wherever you find separation, you will always find the serpent (the devil). I'll leave that there to deal with at another time. You must be able to agree- having the approval of the other person. No man wants to feel like he is standing alone.

Here's a tip to take - agreement always leads to accomplishment - the achievement of a task. Every good and real man wants and knows in this walk we call life he will need a woman he can pray with, and he knows you will pray for him.

I close with this, in the book of Matthew, Chapter 21:22 it says, "And whatever things you ask in prayer believing you will receive." When you have a spiritual connection, there is nothing that can't be done together. Whatever the goal you are striving to reach, keep believing because, in time, it shall be received.

THE

END

FOR NOW!

Chief Editor
Gracia Collins Rich

Amazon Bestselling Author, Gracia Collins Rich is a writer, journalist, and editor. She is a featured writer and contributing editor at Formidable Woman Magazine and a contributing writer for WOE (Women Own Excellence) Magazine and Creating Your Seat At The Table Magazine. You can also find her as a featured blogger on

www.dearshorthair.com, www.thebestiecode.com, www.godandglowing.com, and as a recurring contributing writer for Today's Purpose Woman Magazine.

Gracia's debut thriller, *Handkerchief*, reached #1 on Amazon's Bestsellers list in September 2020. Her writing expertise began with poetry and evolved into short stories, devotionals, and romance. She creates strong, relatable female characters with an edge and endings that are entirely unexpected. Gracia is also a Co-Author of the Glambitous!

Guide to Winning in 2020, as well as the 2018 Anthology, *Letters to Our Daughters.*

Gracia has been featured on IHearThatGirl.com, SwagHer.com, Sheenmagazine.com, Glambitous! Magazine and Courageous Woman Magazine. She is also a Co-host of the Glambitious Podcast.

Gracia is from Rains, South Carolina, the mother of four beautiful children and civil litigation and criminal defense paralegal.